Cupid's Nightmare

Cupid's Nightmare

Atika Desai

For Mom, who deserves the world

1

Meet Cupid

Saturday, January 16

With a firm hold on my shot of chilled water, I took small sips while watching my date from my peripheral vision. He was nothing short of ogling a woman walking past us in a beautiful dress that wrapped her body in a tight embrace. It complimented her voluptuous body and made me feel a ping of envy. She settled down beside me, allowing me to get a better view of the material of the dress under the dim light.

In the midst of trying to conjure up the courage to compliment her and ask her where on God's polluted Earth she got such a ravishing dress…ravishing? God no, who says that? Brilliant? Wonderful? Splendid? Just say beautiful. Just as the courage had been built and my hands reached to touch her shoulders to grab her attention and cop a feel of the sequin, my date cleared his throat.

Startled, I spun on my chair and looked at him with wide eyes. Now, we both got caught ogling the same woman. At least that was one thing we had in common. "Err, what were you saying?"

He jumped off the stool, forcing me to look down at him. "Bathroom break," he said, giving me that simple notice before swaggering off with the pace of a turtle and the limp of someone who lost a leg. He couldn't be bothered to disguise the lustful gazes he threw at the other women in the bar.

There's a reason I preferred going to the bar for a first date, and this was it. Finding out the strength of a man's self-control told a story of its own. As I gathered myself, I'd also leave a story of my own for him to read.

"Bye, Emson!" I called over the music to the bartender who's all too familiar with my antics.

He gave me a lopsided smile and said, "See you next week, Sophia."

I gave him a wide, cheesy smile before hopping off the stool.

The humidity in this place was suffocating and made me tug at my turtleneck. Contrary to popular beliefs, turtlenecks can look great when dressed up well. It's a shame I chose not to care how I looked when I threw it on. Maybe this is why I'd die alone.

With a final glance in the bathroom's direction, I breathed a sigh of relief, glad to see my date's face hadn't popped into sight. Sliding my purse into the crook of my elbow, I made my way out of the bar, the music following me out of the door.

The soft breeze wrapped around me, and the stars winked down at me. The streetlights flickered but still guided me towards an awaiting Toyota car while I reminisced on the seven-minute date with my date whose name was lost in the cool breeze. Seven minutes of pure agony and awkward conversation.

He rolled down the window once I stopped at the passenger door.

"Here for someone?" I asked.

"Sophia Santos," he answered.

Giving him a nod, I opened the back door. "Yep," I answered, popping the 'P'.

As I slid into the back, I glanced outside to steal one more look at the bar but, instead, made eye contact with an awfully familiar man glued to the wall with wide eyes.

I gasped and slammed the door shut, sliding all the way down.

"Go, go, go!" I demanded, burying my face in my hands. It appeared my date also attempted to leave me behind. God, I wanted to disappear into outer space and never meet another man again.

Now, we had two things in common.

When he had driven a safe distance away, my body softened but the daunting thoughts didn't leave. I stretched out my short legs and glanced at the time.

1:15 a.m.

"How's your night been?" he asked when he deemed it safe to talk.

"Pretty good," I said, my lips curving up in an awkward attempt at a smile. Did he know what just happened? Was he playing dumb? "I went on a date."

"And how'd that go?" he asked, continuing to make polite conversation while I rolled down the window. Or maybe he was trying to make me cough up the horrible sin I committed.

Everything passed us in a blur. He drove above the speed limit, but I didn't mind. I just wanted to be curled up in bed in soft pajamas and lull into dreamland. The calming night breeze and empty street did nothing to keep me from nodding off.

"Not good enough. I had to leave him behind."

We made eye contact through the rear-view mirror before his eyes settled on the road again. "That bad?"

"No, he did great," I lied. "He got me flowers, held the door open, was polite, respectful, and was probably going to pay for me." Now that's the truth. He truly did resemble a gentleman up until we sat at the bar. Then, I couldn't even meet his eyes. All confidence I built that morning disappeared. Speaking of flowers, I think I left those behind. What a shame. They were beautiful and smelt fresh too.

"What was the dealbreaker?" he asked.

A genuine smile graced my lips, and I settled back into the comfortable seat. "He's short." Not the dealbreaker, nor did I mind, but what else was I supposed to say? He was busy checking out other women? That's unfair. "Can you turn up the radio, please?" The voices of different artists' filled the car for the rest of the ride.

At last, he pulled up in front of my three-story house, and I said farewell to my driver. One foot after the other, I forced myself up the steps and probed around for my keys until the cool metal met my fingers. Pulling them out, I unlocked the door and let everything but my keychain drop onto the floor the second I stepped inside.

Making use of my functioning body parts, I used my hips to close the door and my hands to unlace my cute flats. My shoulder roamed around the wall, trying to find the light switch while hopping around on one foot. The hallway flooded with light, assaulting my poor eyes, and making me blink away the black dots. I sloppily kicked my flats away with a big, happy sigh while unbuttoning and unzipping my jeans.

I pulled out my phone when it sang with a new message. The screen lit up, showing me a preview of a message.

Unknown: *I miss you*

My lips curled up slightly, and I resisted the urge to write an ill response that would put us back at square one.

"I sure as hell don't miss you," I mumbled.

I swiped the message free from my lock screen, tucked my phone in my pocket, and settled my gaze on my best friend.

"It was a wonderful date," I told my furry friend, Sirus, who greeted me with lazy, slow blinks at the end of the hallway. "I can't wait to see him again! You'll have a step-daddy within weeks now." We met in the middle and turned into the living room. "I think we might get married—"

"You won't be meeting him again because you left before the date even started."

"AHH!" a startled scream ripped through my throat, and I jumped three feet out of my skin. All sleep drained right out of my body, and my senses went into overdrive.

The light in the living room flickered alive, greeting me with the presence of an unknown man. Fear prickled my skin, and I instinctively grabbed my key chain, strangling it in my fist.

"Who are you and what are you doing in my house?"

The stranger looked all too comfortable sitting back on my plush couch with his feet kicked up and drinking from a classy glass that didn't belong to me.

"I'm Cupid." His feet drop from the coffee table with a thump, and he rose to his full height, making me cower back. Even with several feet of space between us, I felt like he loomed over me. "And I'm here to teach you a lesson."

"GET OUT!" the shrill scream echoed through the house, and I'm sure several houses down the street heard it too. I held out my fisted hand, showing him my pepper spray threateningly as it dangled from my key chain. "I'll hurt you."

"No, you won't, Sophia," he said, letting his lips tug up. His deep voice and unwavering gaze made everything seem twice as threatening. "You don't have a harmful bone in your body. Now please, take a seat."

I gaped at him. The nerve of this man to invite me to sit in my own house. "I'm not sitting. I want you out."

"Listen, you're costing me my job, which means I'm not too pleased with you right now—"

"More reason for me to call the police."

"Don't do that," he said when I reached for my phone. "I just want to talk."

"How did you get into my house?" This is the part where I die. I engage foolishly with the predator, he waits for me to drop my guard, and then he pounces. I'm that fool I scream at in movies.

"Simple. You didn't lock the back door."

"Yes, I did..." The argument fell from my lips with passion and anger, but a second later, I realized he's right. The foolish mistake of forgetting to lock the backdoor after allowing Sirus back into the house every morning finally caught up with me in the form of a break-and-enter and maybe even murder. "Wait, did you say you were Cupid?"

"Yes, and that—"

"Then why have I not fallen in love already?" This man is delusional and this whole situation was a mess, but I'm going to make the most of it. Hell, this is the most eventful thing that's happened to me in months. "Did anyone ever tell you you're horrible at your job?" Maybe I should give him a piece of my mind for the trouble he's put me through.

His lips tugged down in a frown, and his dark eyebrows drew in close as he glared at me. "I have a high success rate, thank you very much. Did you ever consider that maybe you're the problem? I've been on your case since you were sixteen, and here we are, a decade later, in the same spot."

My frown mirrored his. "Prove it. Show me your bow and arrow." When I didn't get a reaction out of him, I said, "Considering you're not a baby nor do you have wings, I don't believe you. Get out."

Cupid stared at me for a moment, probably debating on wringing my neck or waterboarding me. "The first date you went on was with Dwayne in high school, and you only did it because you felt left out because everyone else was dating and you weren't."

"Not good enough." It's more than good enough. God, that's a memory so deeply buried, I had to take a moment to recall it. Everyone around me was falling in love, and all I cared for was mastering the art of plucking my unibrow without pulling too much of my eyebrow hairs out. To this day, I still struggle.

"How about that date you went on last year with a married man and when you found out, you told his wife and then proceeded to lock yourself up here for days because you felt like you ruined a marriage?"

That made goosebumps rise on my skin at the memory. I was so deeply ashamed, I told no one about that, not that I spoke to many people, anyway. How did he possess that knowledge?

"Alright, you win," I said at last, dropping my tired arm and tucking away the key chain. I made that too easy for him. "So, why reveal yourself now?"

"Considering I'm getting fired in twenty-nine days if you don't fall in love, I didn't have much of a chose but to meet you in person."

"How do you plan on making me fall in love in twenty-nine days when you couldn't even make me fall in love in ten years?" I sassed.

He glowered at me. "I'm not one of the best for no reason."

"If you were one of the best, you wouldn't be in this position, would you?" .

My statement only managed to intensify his glower, if possible.

"It takes longer than twenty-nine days to fall in love," I pointed out when he said nothing.

He answered reluctantly. "Yes, it does take longer than twenty-nine days to fall in love. But it only takes a few days to feel comfortable with someone and that's all I need you to do. I just need you to form a romantic connection with someone."

"I've had twenty-six years to do that. I hope you're ready to lose your job."

"You should be concerned about me losing my job. If I lose my job, you and the thirty other cases I'm working on will live loveless. Do you want that responsibility?" He smirked victoriously when my face dropped.

"We'll just be reassigned to someone capable of doing their job." Cupid's smirk just widened, telling me that is not the case. "Guess in twenty-nine days, we'll both be miserable."

He breathed in deeply while fishing into his pocket. I eyed his movements, wondering if this was when I would die. Maybe I should have held my tongue and waited until we were in a public setting to backtalk him. He pulled his hand out to reveal a crumpled paper. Gathering his drink, he walked towards me. "You have a date tomorrow. Be there."

After shoving the paper into my fisted hand, he stalked right past me, leaving the lingering scent of musk in his wake. I turned to watch his broad back, making sure he left the house. Once he was safely out of range, I rushed to the door and locked it, followed by the back door. Never again will I make that mistake.

With a threat no longer lingering, a yawn escaped my mouth, reminding me of my comfortable bed. Unable to hold myself up any longer, I leaned back against the wall and pulled out my phone to check the calendar. Twenty-nine days from today would be…I slowly counted my way down the dates until I landed on February 14th. Valentine's Day. I groaned with realization, wanting nothing more than to slam my head against the wall.

Cupid would get fired on Valentine's Day if I didn't get my act right.

Thirty innocent victims and I will die loveless if I didn't get my act right.

Limb by limb, I unglued myself from the wall and forced myself up the stairs and into my room, patiently waiting until I was in my pajamas and lying in bed to open the haphazardly ripped paper I just received.

Lubin Malte

34 Java Street

3:30 pm

A description would have sufficed, but it seemed he liked to be as short with his writing as he was with his words.

Turning on my phone, I opened messages.

Sophia: *I miss you too*

I'd take the worst of the worst if it meant I at least had someone to spend my life with. I knew I couldn't trust Cupid to find me someone compatible.

After turning off the night-lamp, I curled into a ball with Sirus beside me and allowed my mind to wander into a faraway world where love found me.

2

Sugar Daddy

Sunday, January 17

It'd been a while since I'd put effort into my outfit when it came to dates. The dress flowed down to my knees and was paired with cute flats and a simple braid pulled over my shoulder. I even put on a little makeup to tie it all together. I had a good feeling about this one. Cupid did, after all, meet me in person to give me this date.

Upon entering the Uber, I confirmed the address and sat back. The small smile never left, even when the driver almost ran over a pedestrian. It wasn't until he pulled up at my destination that the smile finally crumpled.

"Why are we at a senior's home?" I asked sourly, pinning the driver with an accusing glare as if he set me up on this date.

"That's where the address took us, ma'am," he said politely.

"Well, alright," I said, letting the glare waver. "Thank you for the ride. By the way," I paused on my way out to glance at him, "my grandma's usually out around this time. Be careful and try not to kill her."

His laughter followed me out, abruptly cut off by the door slamming shut. Letting the smile drop, I glared at the beautiful building with budding flowers and decorated windows. I already paid my way here, so there's no going back.

With a deep breath and a word of encouragement, I forced myself into an unfamiliar place to speak to unfamiliar people and navigate my way through unfamiliar halls. Upon entering, I went to the counter and was greeted by a wide smile far too fake to comfort me.

"Hello," I said in response to her greeting. "I'm here for Lubin Malte?"

"What's your name, dear?"

"Sofia Santos."

She searched my name in the database, and I braced myself for rejection. My stomach dropped before she even looked at me. She's going to tell me I was not welcome here, and security would drag me out, kicking and screaming. This was it. This was the first place I would get blacklisted from. This was going to look horrible on my resume.

When she finally looked back at me, the smile was still frozen in place. "Wonderful! I'll get one of the staff to take you to his room!"

I opened my mouth to spill the apology on the tip of my tongue but stopped short. She found me in the database? That should have given me relief, but it only bothered me a little more. Cupid worked magic when he wanted to. Not to mention, if she hadn't found me on the database, I would have a plausible excuse not to go on a date with an elderly man.

Returning her false smile with my own, I turned to the staff she halted. Without hesitation, she took me to the elevators, onto the third floor, and into the left-wing without sharing a word with me.

We walked past the lounging room, where the television played softly. I peered inside and found a few old folks lounging around, but two in particular caught my eye. My steps faltered when my eyes settled on a man delicately holding a woman's hand and shakily putting nail polish on, getting it all over the surrounding skin.

"No, here, like this," she said, using her hand to steady his and guide him.

With a wishful smile and the ache of longing, I picked up my speed and fell into step with the staff. As I replayed the scene, my smile fell, and I winced. There's absolutely no way in hell I'm waiting till the autumn of life to find the love of my life. Not that I'd get that chance anyways if this mission fails.

She led me straight to a room where an elderly man sat on his bed, watching television.

"Hello, Lubin. There's someone here to see you," the woman said in a gentle tone that made it appear as though he were frugal and would break at the touch of a finger. She motioned for me to step in, and I did so while cursing Cupid's name.

He glanced up, his beady eyes running over me in a way that made me squirm. "Sophia," he said at last.

"Lubin," I responded as the staff excused herself.

"Come in and close the door," he instructed, returning his gaze to the muted television.

"How do I know you won't kill me?" I asked with a raised eyebrow. Inching my way forward, I took a swift look around the room. Bland didn't describe just how boring this room was.

"I'm far too feeble for that now."

"That's what they all say." I closed the door, leaving it open just an inch before settling down on the given chair. "Did you know when you watch television, it's more enjoyable if the volume is on and audible?"

His thin lips pressed together, but he continued to keep his gaze steady on the television for a moment longer. Finally, he turned it off altogether and reached for his cane with ease. "Let's dance."

"I don't dance," I told him, staying rooted in my seat as he shakily pulled himself up. I resisted the urge to ask if he needed help. Grandma always hated when I did.

"Well, I do and since you're my date for the afternoon, we're going to dance."

"Hmph," I huffed jokingly. I got to my feet nonetheless and walked over to the classic record player that demanded attention upon first entering. It seemed to be the only personal item in this room.

"Let me do it, girl. You'll only break it." He started to make his way over faster than I thought imaginable for someone his age. They never failed to move fast when their record player was in danger.

"By the time you get here, I'll have put a song on and fallen asleep to it," I teased the grumpy man.

Grabbing the first record, I put it into place and got the music going just as he appeared behind me.

"How did you do that?" he asked in a tone that suggested I did black magic on his precious baby.

"My grandma taught me a thing or two," I said, giving him a small genuine smile at the mention of the old woman. "Now, are you going to teach me how to dance?"

His frown seemed to melt, little by little, the longer we swayed in the open space to the classical music. Intimidating described him best. He had a few inches on me with a grim face and tattoos delicately occupying his leather arms and neck. His firm grip on my waist said anything but feeble, and I didn't doubt that he was capable of murder in his younger years.

"Quit staring at me like that," I said when I met his gaze for the fourth time. I tried my best to avoid looking in his eyes while he tried his best to catch mine. "You're making me fall in love."

I thought I saw a hint of a smile, but it disappeared before I could be sure.

"You're not as bad as Cupid made you out to be," he said at last.

That effectively made me frown. "What has he said about me?"

"You're a stubborn woman who wants a Prince Charming that doesn't exist," he answered as he pulled me deeper into the room.

"That's not true. There are billions of men on this Earth, and you're telling me not one of them is my Prince Charming?"

"You don't want Prince Charming," he advised. He let go of me and reached for his cane. "You weren't lying when you said you can't dance. Put your arms out like a 'T'." I did so. He wrapped one arm under my left armpit and grabbed my other hand with his, bending our elbows a little. "Now move twice to the right and twice to the left. Like this…1, 2, 3, 4," he counted as he swayed me with him, getting me into the rhythm.

I watched the way his hip swayed loosely, and his body moved with the rhythm. The way he moved was nothing short of a dancing leaf in the wind. He seemed more at peace now than he did earlier. His feet moved with such precision and tempo, that in comparison, mine appeared as though they were being dragged through mud. I tried to mimic him but only ended up stumbling and nearly stepping on his toes.

"Why wouldn't I want Prince Charming?" I asked with a slight tilt of my head after I finally found my rhythm. It threw Lubin off for only a millisecond before he adapted to my pace.

"Prince Charming saves damsels in distress. Are you a damsel in distress?" He raised a slow brow, telling me there was only one right answer, and I agreed with him.

"Of course not, but that's not what I mean when I speak about my Prince Charming. I mean someone kind and loving and smart and sweet and…you know, compatible with me."

"Don't forget the part of his name where he's called Charming," Lubin reminded me. "He charms all sorts of women and he knows they're at his mercy. Do you want someone who can smooth-talk you with the same talk he's said to other women?"

"No, of course not," I said at once.

"When the relationship first starts, or even before the relationship, they should be a little nervous around you," he continued. "They should stumble over their words now and again, a twitch of nervousness, and a blush of embarrassment. Be cautioned if a man is always charming and has a greater hold over your emotions than you have over his. It means you're just another girl."

"I guess I've been 'just another girl' for a while now," I mused.

He dropped his hand from under my armpit but kept his firm grip on my other hand still raised and bent in the air between us. "Spin. Turn your right foot and pivot halfway, then use your left to finish turning."

I warily did as told, wondering if I might break his wrist, but he softened his hold and allowed for me to sloppily spin.

"Again."

I tried again and again until I was dizzy and had moderately gotten it down before we were swaying again.

"I'm winded," I said, sucking in a deep breath. "You're far too good at this."

"I know," he said, accepting it more as a fact than praise. "When looking for someone, make sure you're with someone that brings the good out of you."

"Without a doubt," I agreed.

"But don't depend on them to make you a good person," he continued. "You should lean on them but don't depend on them in certain areas. Don't depend on them to bring you happiness or else your life will be dark when they're no longer with you." As he spoke, his eyes seemed to dim slightly, as if he were recalling a loss of his own. "Make sure you have other forms of happiness outside of your partner."

I nodded, drinking in the advice. Sure, I'd heard it all before, but hearing it from a man with great experience felt comforting and wiser. "I won't depend on them for happiness," I promised, "but I can't guarantee that they won't be a source of happiness for me."

"Oh, trust me, they'll be a drug you can't get enough of," he agreed. "If they aren't a source of happiness, there's no reason to keep them around." The light seemed to reappear as he rewarded me with a small, gentle smile. He gazed at me now with kindness, and I think he imagined me to be someone else as his grip became gentle. "And when you find the right one, you'll be more than happy to take the drug and leave yourself vulnerable to them."

The longing in my chest only increased as I witnessed this once-grumpy man now look lost in a world of love of his own. That's what I wanted one day, except I wanted to die before my partner did. I didn't think I'd be strong enough for the heartache. When I expressed this to him, he nodded slowly.

"I don't think she would have been able to handle it well if I left before her," he said, turning thoughtful now. "Little lady, you got me thinking. I've never thought of it that way."

The smile that crawled up my face reflected the accomplishment and pride that made my eyes twinkle.

"Let's do the dip down."

"No!" I cried out, startling both of us. Clearing my throat, I shook my head. "I mean, no. We'll both end up falling."

"We're doing the dip," he said steadfastly, moving his hands to grab both of mine and holding them between us. "Step out."

"This is a bad idea, Lubin," I warned as I stepped back until my arms were extended but his stayed bent.

"Now spin towards me."

He drew a circle with his left arm, pulling me towards him as I spun counterclockwise. "Put both hands around my shoulder." I did so while he put both his arms around my back. It almost felt like an embrace. "Remove your left hand and bend back. I got you."

"You can't even get yourself. You use a cane," I reminded him.

"It's all for show," he said. "Do I look like a man incapable of carrying himself?"

He did have a point there. This whole dance, he'd done well in carrying himself elegantly, never leaning on me once for support. "You sly man," I said with a shake of my head in mock disappointment.

"Make sure you extend your right leg."

Sure enough, he did get me. His arm was strong on my back, and I leaned back, but I must have done it wrong because I felt an uncomfortable pull in my back and my left leg nearly slipped. He pulled me back to my feet before I could fall.

"Ahh, I think I broke my back," I said, moving my hand from his shoulder to touch my lower back.

"You broke your back? I'm the one that had to carry your weight." He stepped away without the use of his cane and sat on his bed, facing me.

"Maybe I should be wary of you. You're just too smooth and charming," I said dryly.

"You should be. I capture all the women's hearts."

I couldn't help a giggle as I sat back down on the chair. The music continued to play on repeat in the background. Even though I was heavy on my feet during the dance, I was as light as a butterfly now, with no weight of the outside world burdening me in this safe space.

I messed around with my phone for a moment, opening the Uber app and closing it a few times. At last, I opened the message I've been ignoring all day.

Unknown: *let's meet Thursday at a place of your choice. You're the only thing on my mind and I need to see you*

Swallowing down my anger, I deleted the whole conversation and tucked my phone away. Lubin would be disappointed if he knew I settled for that thing.

"Am I welcome to stay?" I asked, tilting my head down and fidgeting with my fingers. A part of me feared he'd tell me my time is up and he'd be more than happy to throw me out the window.

"You're more than welcome to stay the whole day," he said, and I didn't fail to take him up on his generous offer.

Who knew this would be my best date?

$$3$$

Cozy with the Enemy

Monday, January 18

Waking up at the beginning of the week knowing I had nothing better to do than spend a good portion of my day at work normally shoved a stick up my bum, but after yesterday, I practically skipped to work and bathed in the warm sun. Nothing could bring me down from Cloud Nine.

Lubin and I spoke for hours about nothing and everything. I told him about my family, and he spoke to me about books and movies we both bonded over. Eventually, we watched a classic movie together and then danced a little more before settling down for takeout food. After that, I said goodnight, promising to come by soon, and then headed back to my lonely home, where Sirus greeted me once more.

If Cupid intended for me to fall in love with elderly people, he shouldn't have wasted his time. My grandmother already taught me that but adding Lubin to the list didn't hurt.

"Sophia!"

Turning around, I glanced back to see who called me, and low and behind, the devil himself showed up. Holding my purse closer to me, I picked up my pace and ducked my head, but it didn't matter. He had already seen me, and he was determined.

His large hand clasped down on my shoulder, and he fell into step with me, syncing perfectly.

"Don't touch me," I snapped, shrugging his hand off.

"This is probably the most action you've got all year," Cupid teased while letting his hand fall to his side.

"No thanks to you." I dodged a bunch of little kids running and squealing past me with backpacks bouncing on their backs as they rushed for school. "So, how does this Cupid thing work?"

"First, tell me how your date went," he said, glancing down at me with a knowing look. It didn't occur to me until now that he probably already got the details from Lubin.

"I thought you wanted me to fall in love, not have a sugar daddy," I said while finally slowing my pace. During my speed walk, my breathing picked up, in contrast to Cupid, who kept pace just fine. Trying to outwalk him did not work.

"Come on," he nudged me. "Tell me the truth."

I gave in. "He was so sweet," I said, glancing up at Cupid. "And he gives great advice. I'm going back for more dancing lessons."

"He is a good dancer," Cupid agreed, tucking his hands into his pockets.

"We even did the dip," I added, hoping he found the information as intriguing as I did when I performed it.

He raised both eyebrows, proving me right. "What?"

"Yeah, he's not as fragile as he appears, but don't tell him I told you. I think it's meant to be a secret," I hurriedly added, realizing I may have given away his identity.

"I already know," Cupid said, waving away my concern. "I'm just surprised he allowed you to know. You must have left an impression."

A wide grin nearly split my face in half. "Oh, I did. I have that effect on people. Although I will say, he's not within my age range, and I don't believe he's emotionally available."

"It's been three years since his wife passed, and he shows no sign of moving on," Cupid enlightened.

"To be fair, I don't think I'd be able to move on too if the love of my life passed," I said honestly. "If that person was nothing but the light of my life, I don't think I'd ever be able to find someone as good, and I don't think I'd even want to try."

"You say that now, but people get lonely, and they start to move on. Sometimes, it's for the better."

When I looked up at him again, I admired how the sun hit him just right, making him glow under the natural light like an angel but with devil's horns. His curly pitch-black hair lightened to a darker brown and fell carelessly over his forehead. He ran his fingers through his shaggy hair and glanced down at me, giving me a better look at his twinkling chocolate brown eyes. It felt like a slow-motion scene right out of a movie.

"You're in a much better mood than you were on Saturday." I blurted the first thing that came to mind and looked away a little too fast.

"On Saturday, I found out I'm one woman away from getting fired. Today, said woman is telling me how great her date went." Cupid flickered my ear playfully, and I couldn't help but let a giggle slip.

"How exactly do you expect me to fall in love when you sent me on a date with a man out of my age range?"

Silence hung between us for a moment, allowing the sound of chirping birds, speeding cars, and talking humans to surround us. I was glad I left for work early or else I would have needed to leave him behind a lot sooner. "It's Ludus love," he answered. "One of the seven Greek loves."

"Why are you teaching me Greek love?" I asked, my eyebrows drawing inwards. My mind flashed to the text I got yesterday and wondered if I should continue to pursue him or trust Cupid, who seemed to have lost his marbles. "I thought—"

"You thought wrong," he cut off. "You're going to need a lot more love in your life than what I can offer, which is Eros love."

"What exactly is Ludus love?"

"Playful love," he said, returning his gaze forward and allowing me a view of his profile. "It's flirtatious and teasing love. It's simple love that's meant to be fun without the need for security or a long-withstanding relationship."

"Lubin and I did not flirt," I stated. "But I can't say I didn't have fun talking to him and learning to dance."

"Then I did a great job," he answered, giving me a wink.

"You're still not that good at your job. Don't get too cocky," I said in an attempt to humble him.

"I'm the greatest you'll ever meet. I give the real ancient Cupid a run for his money—watch out." Cupid wrapped an arm around my shoulder, and we both flew to the side, straight into the rough bricks of a building as a skateboarder out of control zapped past us.

We glanced back in time to see him slip right off and fall on his bum as his skateboard continued forward with a mind of its own. Before I could express concern, he was already on his feet and chasing his board.

"Whoa," I whispered, gazing up at Cupid through my lashes. He redirected his attention to me. "You saved my life." I batted my eyes and pouted my lips in a mock attempt at friendly, funny flirting.

That successfully got me a smile that showed a slight gap between his front teeth. I swooned and practically turned into a puddle. Gap teeth always got me, and this sucker knew it.

"I sure did, Princess," he said, deepening his voice. "You can thank me later."

"Oh." I fanned my face with my hands, letting a giggle slip. "How?"

"By going on this next date." He pulled a paper out of his pocket and once more slipped it into my hand. "Have a good day, love," he said in an awful British accent. With a short bow, he took his leave, allowing my laughter to trail after him.

The wide grin dropped as fast as it appeared, leaving me gaping at his back when Cupid knocked his shoulder into a well-suited man, forcing him to drop his briefcase and pop open. Cupid didn't even bother glancing back or apologizing. I pushed off the wall, ready to offer the man help, but another woman closer to him beat me to it.

"Thank you," he said, looking up to thank the woman. "Maria?"

"Juan! My god, it's been so long!" the woman said, her eyes the size of gold balls, not believing the sight in front of her. "Holy shit, how are you?"

Sliding my eyes away from them, I searched for Cupid, and sure enough, I found him at a cross light. As if feeling my gaze, he turned his head and met my eyes. All I received was a simple wink before he headed off to continue with his day while I continued to stare with a slacked jaw.

4

Barf Color

Wednesday, January 20

Centered right in the middle of the week was when Cupid deemed it appropriate for my next date. I couldn't say I wasn't excited. If it went anything like the first one, I'd have someone to eat dinner with.

"Hey, Mom," I greeted over the phone. "How's everything been?"

"Can't complain," she said. "How about you? What have you been up to?"

I put the phone on speaker so I could multitask. "Nothing really," I lied. It was pointless to tell her I was going on a date and get her hopes up. I think as the years stretched on, they came to accept that I wasn't going to bring a man home any time soon.

"Nothing, nothing, nothing," Mom mocked. "That's all you ever do. Do you never leave the house?"

"I actually left the house this morning," I argued.

"Work doesn't count," she argued back. I could hear running water in the background and drew a logical conclusion.

"What's that sound? Is someone trying to drown themselves?"

"I'm doing the dishes. Why would you possibly think someone was trying to drown? Would I be having a calm conversation with you if that was happening?" she asked in an exasperated voice.

"I don't know. We're all kind of twisted."

"You're the only twisted one. You must have been switched at birth. I refuse to believe you're my daughter," she berated.

"Mother, why must you hate your only daughter? Am I not good enough for you?"

"You aren't my only daughter, and that's why it's easy to hate you," she said playfully.

"Oh right, I forgot about that puta, Elena." I waited for her to chastise me for calling my sister such an insult, but it appeared Mom wasn't familiar with Spanish.

Elena had it all. She was the golden child, leaving me behind to be the disappointing other daughter. Even with three stupid brothers who were easy to outshine, I somehow still managed to be pushed into their shadows.

"Anyways, we're having a family dinner this Saturday and if you don't come, I'll send your siblings to drag you here, alright?"

"You say that as if I always make excuses to not come or just don't show up at all," I said, pursing my painted lips.

"Because you do," she said flatly. "Anyways, make sure you're here by seven or come earlier. I miss you." Guilt settled in the pit of my stomach.

"I miss you, too. I'll be there. Anyways, I have to go. Love you."

"Love you, too."

Now, it was time for my date. Hopefully, this would go well so that I could take him to the family dinner. Maybe that would get the relationship moving and we could be married by next month.

Tucking my open hair behind my ear, I got into the Uber and confirmed the address. Clearly, I hadn't learned my lesson the first time because I didn't check to see where I'd be heading. When she pulled up at a spa, relief passed over me; at least it wasn't a graveyard. I wasn't sure how I'd take it if I had to talk to the dead.

"Thank you!"

Once I stood outside, I pulled out my phone and called my date with the number Cupid had the courtesy of giving me this time.

"Hello?" a high-pitched, feminine voice greeted me.

"Hi, can I talk to Alex?"

"This is her!" I turned to my left and saw an overly enthusiastic women with a phone pressed to her ear smiling at me. "Is this Sophia?" she asked over the phone as we stood two feet away from each together.

I resisted the urge to purse my lips while I mentally cursed Cupid. We both ended the call and met in the middle.

"Hey," I said to the preppy woman highlighted in pink. Pink top, pink bow, pink eyeliner, pink nails. "Yeah, I'm Sophia."

"I love your hair! It's so shiny and straight," she complimented. I couldn't help but give her a wide smile of my own.

"Thanks, I get it from my mom. Wanna know a secret? I use horse shampoo. It keeps my hair from falling off." Right now, despite my instant liking for her, I wanted nothing more than to rip my hair off my head. Cupid was playing a game he couldn't win.

"You'll have to tell me how you take care of your curls. I heard it's a difficult process."

"Oh, I'll tell you all about it while we get our nails done. I hope you don't mind. Cupid mentioned that you don't take care of yourself, so I figured we'd start with your nails." Upon seeing my jaw hanging, she quickly added, "But I will admit, you look very well taken care of. Cupid can be spiteful when he's angry."

"I hope Cupid also knows I'm not into women," I said with a small shrug and apologetic smile.

"Oh, he knows," she said and, with a wave of her hand, threw away my concern. "Don't worry about that."

We entered, and she gave her name and reservation to the man at the front. After a short conversation that told me they were well acquainted, we walked past a few people getting their nails done, and my eyes lingered on the bickering couple.

"I told you we were going to my parents' house for the weekend," she snapped, glaring at him. The nail artist frowned when she snatched her hand away and accusingly pointed at her husband. "You always do this."

"I didn't do it on purpose," he snapped back but sat perfectly still, much to the gratitude of his nail artist. "I thought you said we were going to my parents' place."

"How, DJ? How is that possible when we already went last week? You know we alternate. I swear you do this on purpose…"

Their conversation faded off when Alex and I entered a private room that broke first date budget by a mile. Before the door closed, I stole one last glance at the couple. The woman still had a frown plastered but it wavered the more her husband poked and teased her with a few apologies in between. Arguments and bickering can't be escaped, no matter how loving the relationship is. Despite past relationships, I had yet to be in a simple argument like what I witnessed without it ending with me in tears and begging for forgiveness. It was a reoccurring problem in my last relationship.

As we settled in, just the two of us waiting for the nail technician, she asked, "What have you been up to?"

I hated that question with a passion. It was hard to make my life seem interesting when there was nothing interesting about it. "I'm a web designer and work downtown. And I, uh…" When I struggled to add something else, she jumped in.

"Downtown, huh? Do you drive?"

"No, I don't own a car. It's useless since a lot of things are within walking distance and I just take the subway to work, which only takes me half an hour," I said, watching as she twirled her fingers around her long hair. Even with it up in a ponytail, it still reached her hips. "Are you wearing extensions, or do you just take great care of your hair?"

"Okay, listen," she said, leaning forward. "I hate extensions with a passion, so I'm grateful I'm able to grow my hair out this long. Do you understand what a hassle it is getting fake hair into your own hair and then struggling to hide the band while you can't even hold your arm up for more than two minutes?"

I nodded my head sympathetically. "I tried doing Dutch braids before, but I never succeeded because my arms always get sore before I can ever pick up three strands."

"Oh, I love Dutch braids. Once you get the hang of it, it's great. Let me braid your hair right now!" she said excitedly, pleading me with her wide hazel eyes.

"Yes please," I said without hesitation.

She moved to the chair that the nail technician used, and I sat on the floor, fitting myself between her long, slender legs. The jeans hugged her just right, and I admit to checking out her perky butt when she walked ahead of me earlier. She clearly took great care of herself. I could see the faint hint of abs her crop top didn't cover.

As she started to work skillfully at the top of my skull, I asked, "One day, you'll have to do my makeup as great as you do yours." And then I winced. Stupid, stupid, stupid. Who said she wanted to hang out with you again?

She didn't miss a beat. "Honey, I will do your make up all the way until your wedding and then some. Then, I'll start doing your daughter's makeup, ya hear?"

Letting out a soft breath, I smiled. I could see myself being best friends with her. "I hear," I said. "Thank you."

By the time she was done, the nail technicians finally walked in, and we both went back to our respective chairs.

"Hey, Cece! Hey, Olah!" Alex greeted the two women around our age.

"What up, G?" Olah said, sitting in front of Alex while Cece sat in front of me.

"Hey," Cece said meekly.

"Meet my date, Sophia," Alex introduced, and I gave a wave with a polite smile.

Olah raised her chin at me and Cece gave me a timid smile.

The two women were polar opposites of each other, and adding Alex to the mix, it wasn't hard to say they were a diverse group of friends. Alex had the preppy cheerleader look and personality down.

Cece not only seemed like a sweet, shy person, but her short, bony frame that her oversized shirt dwarfed only added to her timid persona. If Cece weren't introduced, she would have blended right into the background and I wouldn't have noticed her past Olah's demanding presence.

Olah walked with a swagger and a cocky smirk. With her scuffed-up shoes and finger tattoos, she looked ready to rough up anyone who so much as gave her a wrong look. Her broad frame told me she played sports in her free time and loved working out.

"Cute date," Olah said as they both gathered their utensils. "A word of advice, the girl's nuts. Run as fast as you can." Despite how scary she looked, her smile said otherwise, and she radiated kindness.

As I laughed, Alex shot her a dirty look. "Don't say that, and besides, we're more on a platonic date than a romantic date."

"Fitting," Olah said. "I've known Alex since birth, and I swear her first words were platonic."

"No, her first words were 'the quadratic equation,'" Cece said in a level voice just below normal tone. Our eyes met and we shared a grin.

"To be fair, my brother's first word was 'inverse function,'" I said. "If only he was a girl."

"If only," Alex said with a dreamy sigh.

"What color do you want?" Cece asked.

"The ugliest one," I said, briefly glancing at the color book. "I want to make Cupid vomit when he sees it."

"Oh," Olah said with a knowing look. "You're Cupid's nightmare, huh?"

"Cupid told you about me also?" I asked, exhausted. How many people knew me as some stupid, dirty girl because Cupid couldn't keep his mouth shut? "Isn't that a breach of privacy or something?"

"Probably," Olah said.

"It is," Cece said with certainty as she got to filing my nails.

"But one thing you'll find tis Cupid does not care about rules," Olah said, shaking her head. "That boy is damned."

"But he's sweet," Cece kindly intervened. "He brings us donuts when we work the weekend."

"He spits in them first," Alex said with a crackle. "I've seen him do it."

"Only on the ones he knows Olah will eat," Cece said with a small smile. "She has a way of getting under his skin."

"Who doesn't like a little spit in their donut?" Olah said, making us all laugh.

When the light banter slowed down, all attention fixed on me.

"So," Alex started, "Cupid says you've never given a man the time of day. How true is that?"

I frowned. "Not true at all. All I do is give men the time of day to waste and disappoint me."

"Amen," Cece whispered.

"To be fair, if he meant I've never fallen in love with any of them, he's completely right. Tell me I'm not abnormal," I pleaded, looking among the three woman I'd already found myself comfortable with.

They all mumbled a response, avoiding eye contact.

"Alright, fine, so it's a little abnormal," I grumbled, staring down at my nails that Cece was intensely working on. "Maybe I'm just incapable of love."

"Not possible," Olah declared. "We're all capable of love, especially falling in love with strangers and wanting to make them our future spouse. Your standards just touch the sky, and you're not willing to settle for less, which is great."

"Oh please, my sister has standards higher than me, and once, she fell head-over-heels for some bum who smoked weed day in and day out." Saying it out loud only made me sadder. "I'm too old to still be searching."

"Please," Alex scoffed. "You're hardly old. People have found love in their forties and fifties."

I winced.

"Wait, wait, wait!" Alex cried. "I'm not saying that'll be you! I'm just saying don't give up."

"Cupid told us your last relationship ended horribly," Cece said, peering up at me. "Wanna talk about it?"

"I've only been in four relationships. The first one was purely because I didn't want to feel left out. The second one lasted a month, and I couldn't bring myself to stay any longer when I found out he eats his boogers. The third one lasted a week, and we broke up because he told me I had nice hair—"

"What?" Alex asked, her eyes widening. "But I said that."

"Yeah, well, I prefer it from everyone but him. I swear he collected hair for a living or something." That made them all laugh.

"No wonder Cupid says you're a nightmare. You pick out the smallest thing and refuse to make it work," Olah said, her eyes still sparkling with amusement.

I shamefully nodded my head. "I went on a date last week, and it didn't last a minute because he didn't hold the door open for me. I just left."

"I would too," Cece agreed.

"One time a guy spat water on me on our first date because he saw something funny," Olah started. "We dated for three months."

Cece and Alex nodded their head, approving the story.

"God no," I said with a cringe. "I would have walked right out."

"He was good in bed," Alex said with a smirk. "Or so she says."

Olah just shrugged with a massive grin, her eyes glazing over.

Cece paused her work on my hand and caught my eyes. "You're scared of love, aren't you?"

"What? No. I long for it," I argued, my eyebrows shooting up.

"What're you scared of, Sophia?" Alex said, but her tone was teasing and kind.

We sat in silence as I pondered the question. Scared? Why would I be scared of love when it's all I've been seeking? "Maybe I'm scared of picking the wrong person."

"Ditto to that."

"Amen, sister."

"Say it louder."

As we got our nails done, we laughed and joked, and I listened to them ramble about their problems. They treated me like I've been their friend for years, and it made my heart feel lighter. The weight of the world didn't feel so heavy.

5

Reality Check

Slumping down on my chair on the front porch, I glared down at my phone when it continued to ring for the third time.

"Shut up, alright?" I hissed, turning off the volume. "Get the hint."

He didn't get the hint.

When the call ended, it took ten seconds before it started ringing again. "Oi, shut up!" I snapped, flipping the phone over and directing my glare ahead of me. "Oh my god," I gasped, putting a hand on my chest when I found someone standing at the foot of the steps, staring at me with a small smile and their phone to their ear.

"Ignoring me?"

"Uh…Thor! How did you—when did you—no, I wasn't, it's just…hey, how are you?" I pushed my hair over my shoulder as the heat caught up with me and the blazing sun set me on fire.

Thor, my fourth and final relationship.

"I'm good," he answered, soundlessly walking up the steps and sitting down beside me without a peep. For a man as big as him, it was impressive. "Any particular reason you stood me up?"

"Well, I didn't stand you up. I never confirmed to going on the date," I reminded him, shifting my chair to the side.

"Are you upset at me?" He shifted in his chair, so he faced me now, and his beautiful aqua eyes held mine in a curious gaze. "Sophia, I know we left on bad terms, but I've changed now. It's been almost two years since we last saw each other. I thought you forgave me."

Four years since we broke up in my last year of university and two years since we last met in person, where I reluctantly accepted his apology for being the worst boyfriend on the face of the Earth. We texted on and off, but it's been a year since I last heard from him. Until recently, that is.

"Yes, I did forgive you," I admitted while nodding my head as guilt settled on my shoulders, making me slump forward. I had no reason to be so petty. "I'm sorry, Thor. I've just been busy with a few things and a little stressed, so I guess I wasn't in the best mindset to meet or talk to you." I blinked at him, hoping he accepted my pathetic apology.

He gave me a small smile, his eyes lightening with happiness, and put his rough hand on my thigh, giving it a soft squeeze. The small gesture made my insides warm and I placed a hand over his.

"Don't worry about it," he assured me. "We all have those days."

My smile widened, glad to be forgiven for a stupid mistake. "How have you been, Thor?"

"This life is a blessing," he admitted with gratitude. "Mom recently got out of the hospital after a car accident—"

I gasped. "Is she okay?"

"Yes, yes," he assured me, "she's doing great. I've been staying with her for the past few days to look after her and take care of her, but thankfully, it wasn't anything life threatening."

"Thankfully," I mumbled in agreement.

He fished around in his pocket, and when he pulled his hand out, he held a fun-sized Mars Bar. My smile lifted when he put it in front of me.

"You still remember?" I asked, a little touched.

"How could I forget?" he asked, placing a hand over his heart in mock offense. "It was my little weapon I used to calm you down when you got hysterical."

"Only because you'd push me over the edge," I reminded him, not letting my smile waver.

He ran his fingers through his soft, silky hair and gave me his famous dimpled smile. "You're right."

That softened the hard edges of my smile. "I know," I said jokingly, bumping my shoulders against his. "But I guess we just needed time away from each other to heal."

"We did," he agreed. "We were just two lost kids battling their own problems and taking it out on each other, but I don't regret the time I had with you. The way I see it, right person, wrong time."

I slowly nodding my head, wondering if that really was the case. I sure hope so.

"Anyways, how are you? What have you been up to?"

I gave him the basic, boring run down, but he probed a little more, insisting that something interesting must be going on. I finally cracked because Thor was a good listener and I needed an unbiased opinion right now.

"There's this guy, Cupid, who basically controls my love life. Don't ask me how, I don't know. Anyways, if I don't fall in love within the next twenty-something days, he's going to be jobless and I'm going to be loveless for the rest of my life, along with thirty other people because…"

I rambled on and on, trying to convince him of the severity of the situation, and he listened with narrowed eyes and understanding nods. He occasionally raised an eyebrow and I'd elaborate, but for the most part, he knew what I was saying before I said it. He understood me to my core.

When I finished, he said, "Cupid doesn't exist, Sophia. It's just a myth."

I knew better than to argue with him. "You think?"

"I know," he said. "I want you to be careful. I would hate to see anything to happen to you, and if you ever need me, I'll always be here for you, alright?"

"Thank you," I whispered.

"This guy is some sort of scam. I'd call the police if I were you, alright? Put some sort of restraining order on him and don't worry so much. You're still young, and there's still a lot of time before you have to settle down. Just have fun."

"I really needed that," I admitted, realizing how stupid I had been. "Thank you, Thor."

"Hey, you can say thank me by promising to meet me again," he said with a playful poke to my side that made me giggle and sway a little.

"Okay, promise."

We talked for a while longer after that, mainly about recent television shows and what he'd been up to. I didn't have much to say about myself, and I didn't mind hearing about his great successes. Turns out, he's been running a charity to sponsor girls for school in developing countries. In the past, he'd raised over 4,000 dollars for wildlife. I listened with wide eyes, envisioning a future where we worked side by side on such progressive, rewarding projects.

No word in the 6, 500 languages spoken in this world would ever be able to describe how great this man was. I guess people can change.

Cupid may get to keep his job after all.

6

Explosive Diarrhea

Thursday, January 21

"Hi, babe. How was your nap?" I greeted Sirus, who jumped on the dining chair and watched me with wide, curious eyes as I grabbed ingredients to start on dinner. She meowed, and I nodded in understanding. "Yeah, must be nice. I should start taking afternoon naps again."

She meowed in agreement and continued to watch me flawlessly move around the kitchen.

The kitchen is my safe haven. While the mortgage still needs to be paid off, I couldn't resist the temptation of renovating the kitchen and I didn't regret it one bit. This was the one place I moved effortlessly and knew exactly where everything was, right down to the grain of salt on the floor an inch away from the left corner of the stove. This was the place I poured my heart into when I was happy or sad or angry and everything in between. No one could take this away from me. Not even my mind, which had isolated me from friends and family on many occasions.

After Thor left, I lounged around inside the house, pondering over his words for a while and concluded that there's no way Cupid is fake. Why would he drag it on for this long with convincing evidence to support him? Not to mention the several people he'd set me up with, all for my benefit. I decided to put Thor's thoughts on hold for a while.

With him no longer in my presence, the adoring fog in my mind that blinded me to all the reasons we broke up cleared. It reminded me of the promise I engraved into my mind after we broke up. Every morning, for about two weeks, I would stare myself down in the mirror with my red-rimmed eyes glaring right back as I promised myself that no one would tear me down until I was nothing but tears and a hollow shell of skin and flesh, contemplating my worth and debating my existence. Allowing one man to do it was enough for several lifetimes.

Sharp knocking on the back door disturbed my depressing thoughts and nearly made me lose bowel control. Letting out a shaky breath that shook my whole body, I grabbed my butcher knife and edged towards the sliding glass door. The closed curtains prevented me from peering outside to see who could be intruding at such an hour.

"Open the door, Sofia," a familiar, muffled voice called, making me instantly relax.

Pulling back the curtain and unlocking the glass room, I slid it opened and greeted Cupid with a glare.

"You couldn't use the front door like a normal human?" I growled, stepping aside to let him in. A breeze of mild winter air entered with him, and I found myself wanting to eat outside now. For a moment, I wished I lived in the north to experience the extreme cold weather and fluffy snow."

"Sorry," he said with a careless shrug. "I figured the back door would be open."

"You can't keep breaking into my house," I countered, pointing the knife at him.

He ignored me and sat down on the dining chair beside Sirus, who got to her paws and climbed onto his thighs. That traitor. I glared at her, silently trying to communicate my hurt while she just stared at me with half-open eyes as Cupid petted her.

"I like your nails," Cupid said, looking at my perfectly manicured fingers. Despite asking Cece to give me the ugliest color, she painted them ombre pink and red, telling me Cupid shouldn't be the reason I walked around with ugly nails. I found it ironic that she painted them the famous Valentine's color that reminded me of nothing but Cupid.

My lips tipped up, and I momentarily got distracted staring at the glossy finish. "Right? Cece has talent."

"Speaking of, how was your date?" Cupid asked.

"You should probably add this to your file: I'm not lesbian," I said flatly, returning to my meal.

"Noted," he said with a slight nod and a soft upwards curve of his lips. "But really, how'd you find it?"

"It was great," I said reluctantly. "We laughed a lot and they treated me like a real friend. It makes me miss university when I had friends."

"What happened to them?" he asked curiously, but something told me he already knew. I'd be surprised if he didn't know.

With a slight tilt of my head, I returned to my station in the kitchen. My mouth opened and closed, trying to find the right words to explain what happened.

"I pushed them away," I said at last. "Remember my last relationship in university?"

Cupid hummed.

"I'm sure you know just how toxic it was."

Cupid hummed again.

"He was controlling and manipulative and a pathological liar, but you know what's funny?"

"What?"

"The first three months we were together, he was sweet and funny, and he really seemed like he cared about me, so why did I never fall in love with him? In fact, why have I never fallen in love? Am I incapable of it? Will I die alone?" I asked the questions that had weighed on me for a while now. It seemed damn near impossible for me to feel anything past infatuation, if I even stay long enough to catch those feelings. I was convinced I was a robot that bled, but Mom showed me the video of her giving birth to me and debunked my theory. I wish she would have debunked it differently.

"No, you just haven't found your match," he answered smoothly, not missing a beat just like the Mr. Perfect he was. "You're capable of love. You love your family and your cat."

"It's not the same as being in love."

"Yes," he agreed. "And you'll experience it soon enough."

All he got was a *hum* in response to his answer. The answer wasn't satisfying enough. It did nothing to dispel the thought of dying alone.

"So, you have no friends?" he asked, filling the silence with a seemingly harmless question.

I shrugged, trying to bury my embarrassment. "Just the ones at work," I admitted in a mumble.

"It's okay," Cupid said. "You have Alex now."

"Yeah, we made plans to hang out next week, so that should be fun." I was grateful for that. They wanted to go to the theaters on Tuesday and watch the new horror film. They were more than happy to have me come along and I couldn't bring myself to say no, not that I wanted to anyways. I hadn't been to the theaters in a while.

"So, what kind of love was that?"

"It's Philia love, which is the love of the mind. It's catered towards plutonic and sincere love, usually made with siblings or friends, in which you can openly express yourself and have a meaningful conversation," he spieled with perfection, as if he had practiced in the mirror before coming here.

"I like this one."

While grating the cheese, I was drawn to look at him once more.

I'd die before I openly admitted that Cupid was an attractive man. That man oozed with cockiness and I didn't want to encourage it, but I was allowed to admit it to myself. His biceps called me weak as they flexed while petting my purring kitty. They were well defined and inviting all attention to the short-sleeved shirt, compared to his usual long-sleeved ones. His scruffy beard didn't hide his uneven jaw too well, but I doubt many people noticed. I couldn't nail Cupid to one look, but it had to be somewhere between someone you wouldn't introduce to your parents and the boy next door look. His resting face wasn't pleasant and hinted at murder, but the second his lips tilted up and his eyes softened, he seemed like an innocent, sweet man that's just misunderstood. An innocent murderer fitted him well.

"I have a few pictures of myself naked that I can send you if you'd like," Cupid said without looking up.

Flames licked every surface of my body, and I quickly redirect my gaze, holding the cheese even tighter.

"I was more impressed with your ability to tame my cat," I lied. "Your biceps have nothing on mine."

He looked up, and I flexed my fat for him, receiving a chuckle that ran down my spine and made me stand a little taller. He raised in hands in mock surrender, eyeing my arms with stars in his eyes. "Wow, I wish that was me."

Returning to grating the cheese, I said, "I can give you a few tips."

"Please do, oh master of muscles." He clasped his hands together in front of his face, and I'm sure he'd get on his knees if it wasn't for Sirus. "I'm begging!"

Unable to help it, I threw my head back and laughed a loud, belly laugh that cut short before it could fully leave my chest. The cheese in my hand snapped in half, and my fingers were instantly sliced by the sharp blade.

"Oh man," I hissed, dropping everything and pulling away from the cheese so I wouldn't get blood on it.

"Are you alright?" The smile slipped from his face in an instant. He gently put Sirus down, who glared at me accusingly, before rushing to my side.

"Yes, yes," I said, waving him away. He didn't budge. He turned on the water for me and asked where the first aid kit was. "Over there." While he looked for it, I ran my fingers under the water. I inspected my fingers and found a few scratches. My middle finger got the worst of it. "I hope you like blood in your food. I heard it brings out the flavor."

"Sophia Santos," Cupid said, walking over to me with the first aid kit. "Did you just invite me for dinner?"

For the second time tonight, my face reflected a tomato. I had to give him credit. It'd been a while since someone had made me blush like this, and Cupid was the last person I expected to achieve it. "No, I take it back," I said, wildly shaking my head. "It was the loss of blood talking."

"Mm," he hummed sarcastically. "Let me see the cut."

"I can wrap it just—"

"Let me see it," he said, his voice dropping an octave. On their own accord, my hands reached out and allowed him to see the damage.

When the spell wore off, I gasped. "Cupid!" I lightly slapped his arm with my free hand. "Don't ever use that tone with me again."

"What tone?" he asked, playing dumb. He wiped the cut with disinfectant and then tore open a band-aid.

"That—that—ugh, you know what I'm talking about. That authoritative tone. It struck the fear of God in me," I admitted.

"What can I say?" he asked. "I'm the devil and angle combined." That described him perfectly. "All new."

I inspected my hand and his crafty, flawless job of wrapping my finger so delicately. I hardly felt it. "I'd say you're only the son of Satan without a hint of an angel in you."

He moved past me to wash his hands. "What are we eating tonight?"

"Pizza," I answered. "And we can eat outside if you'd like. It's nice out."

"I don't mind," he said. After wiping his hands, he started grating the cheese while I started on the tomato sauce.

"So, how does the whole Cupid thing work? You clearly aren't the son of Mercury and Venus," I eyed him. "Are you?" Even though I believed he needed to set me up with a partner and called himself Cupid, Thor did have a point. Cupid is a myth.

"Nope." He popped the 'P'. The word rolling off his tongue effortlessly and past his plump, pink lips perfectly. It reminded me of the smile we shared earlier, and I wanted to see it again just so I could get a peek of his gapped teeth. "They're my great-great-great-great-great-great-great-great-great-great-great-great-great—"

"I get it," I said dryly.

"—Grandparents. Over time, immortality was no longer granted and as they started to mate with humans, there were more average babies than mythical ones. I know it's hard to tell, but I'm the average one."

"Yep," I bounced my head up and down, "super hard to tell."

"I think it's the fact that I'm irresistible that gets people confused," he continued, throwing me a boastful smirk. "Or maybe it's the incredible, out-of-this-world good looks." He wiggled his eyebrows, and I pressed my lips together to suppress a giggle.

"Now that's where I draw the line." I put a hand on my hip and gave myself an excuse to check him out. "I've met far more attractive men than you."

"Oh yeah?" he asked, turning his full attention to me and raising a challenging brow. "Name one."

"You know that guy that went viral for saying 'Deez nuts'? Him," I said with a satisfied smile. That should humble him.

"Yeah?" he asked again, his eyebrows raising even higher, if possible. "Okay, I'll make a note of that. You'll be more than impressed with your upcoming date."

"No!" I cried, nearly lunging for him as he pulled out his phone. "No, beautiful Cupid. There is no one as great or as smothering as you." That's not to say that the 'Deez nuts' man is ugly, but he's just not my type.

"Smothering?" he asked, squinting his almond shaped eyes at me. "Never heard that one before, but if you insist." He bowed his head and put a hand over his heart. "I'm truly flattered."

"Har har," I laughed sarcastically before we resumed working. "Tell me more about Cupid."

"Well, instead of just being one man who's in control, there's a bunch of us all over the world who have taken the responsibility of finding compatible people and making them fall in love. We're all extended family of the original Cupid and all hoard the power of sensing unique love. We dedicate our lives to this job."

"It must feel rewarding when you pair couples who will spend the rest of their lives together," I mused softly. "But what about the flip side? Must suck when you put so much time into a great couple, only to have them divorce or break up."

He shook his head. "Then we never set them up. At least, for the most part, we didn't. Humans are still capable of choosing their destiny and breaking free from the unknown power, which we have. We test them with a few people to see who they're compatible with and then pull the trigger that makes them fall in love but sometimes, they fall in love before they're supposed to. While it can be frustrating, it is also encouraged because it teaches them about heartbreak and love and how to pick a better partner in the future."

"And how can you get fired from the job?" Was that possible? If you're born with an inevitable power, you couldn't really get fired from a job.

"Happens to the best of us." He shrugged. "The committee is coming down harder on me because I fool around too much and they want me out, but I'm not going down without a fight."

"Ah, you don't like rules," I said, recalling Olah's words.

"Exactly. Been doing your research on me?" We were close enough for him to be able to lightly nudge me.

"Don't flatter yourself," I said and bit my lips to suppress another giggle.

"Come on, laugh," he encouraged. "I know you want to." He finished with the cheese, and his hands were now free so when he extended them towards me, I knew exactly what he planned.

"Cupid, don't do it!" I cried. Before I could move away, he grabbed hold of me and tickled me under the arms. "No!" I squirmed away from him, laughing. "Don't be rude!"

His chest moved up and down with his vibrant laughter, ringing through the kitchen and lightening the already bright room. The house filled with the sound of laughter that wasn't mine, and it added a touch of warmth and a splash of color to the house. I think the house was smiling too, grateful for some positive energy.

My mood dampened as realization dawned on me: I was lonelier than I let on, living in a three-story house with no one to share it with. The accomplishment did nothing to raise my mood because I had no one to share my victory with. I had pushed friends away, and my family dropped by every few months, if ever. I had chosen this life for myself, and I hated it.

When Cupid left, so would the laughter and happiness.

Cupid's smile dimmed as he noticed mine slip off my face. "Are you—"

I forced the grin back in place and resumed working. "Can you preheat the oven, please?"

For the remainder of the cooking, I spoke little to him. Cupid picked up on it but didn't excuse himself as I had hoped. No, he was determined to eat dinner and then leave.

Since I was making two small pizzas, I decided to add a touch of love to his tomato sauce. The pizza was baking in no time since I made the dough earlier this morning before heading to work. While we waited, Cupid and I sat in the living room and watched whatever played on the television. Or at least, he watched, and I went through my phone.

The buzzer went off, forcing me to my feet and into the kitchen. I cut both pizzas into four slices, put them onto a plate, and headed outside to eat with Cupid. We settled into the seats on the front porch, where the heavenly smell of jasmine greeted us. Gardening was a nightmare, but all my life I'd grown up with jasmine plants and couldn't resist the urge to grow one myself.

"Mm, this is good," Cupid complimented. His shoulder brushed mine, and his warmth wrapped around me. Resisting the urge to lean in closer proved hard.

"I know," I said, feeling the flutter of butterflies in my stomach at the compliment. "My grandma taught me. It's my favorite recipe. Had I known you'd be eating dinner here, I would have also made apple pie."

"You should stop hitting on me, Sophia," Cupid said, brushing his hair out of his eyes and giving me a cocky grin.

I giggled and shook my head. "Shut up. I just really like cooking and baking for people. I don't get to do it often, so it's nice when I have company."

"If you want me over for dinner again, just ask. You don't have to hint at it." He chuckled when I glared at him.

"You're too cocky for your own good, you know that?"

"Women adore it," he said, lifting a heavy shoulder in a shrug and sliding me a sexy smirk. "What's a trait you like in men?"

"Oh, is Cupid flirting with me?" Grateful that the attention was no longer on me, I switched to teasing him.

"I need to know who to set you up with," he answered, relaxing into his chair. "You're a hard one to crack open."

We joked some more, and after we were done eating, we settled into calm silence, enjoying each other's presence and the sound of occasional passing cars, chirping crickets, and faint laughter. I turned to look at Cupid, wanting to ask him something…something that seemed so important and urgent just a moment ago but as soon as I realized how close my face was to his, my mind flat-lined.

Cupid tilted his head towards me, giving me his wholehearted attention. His eyes held mine in a comforting way, silently urging me to ask whatever it was I wanted to ask. I bit my bottom lip and realized how dry they were. His eyes flickered down to look at them. His breath brushed against my face, warming me more than I already was. His chest moved up and down in even rhythms and…was he moving towards me?

His calm body suddenly shifted away from me, and he closed his eyes. I reeled back and wrapped my arms around my stomach, turning away from him too. From the corner of my eyes, I noticed he started squirming and just like that, my embarrassment disappeared as I realized what was happening.

"What's wrong?" I asked with mock concern when he wouldn't let up.

"Nothing," he said, rising to his feet. "I should get going now. Thanks for dinner, Sophia."

"Wait, I need to give you something. Come inside."

"Can it wait?" he asked, shifting from one foot to the other, as he clenched his jaw and forcefully swallowed. "I need to go."

"No, no, I need to give it to you right now," I insisted, grabbing his forearm and pulling him towards the house. Of course, he didn't budge, but with a little more pleading, he shuffled his feet and followed. I could see sweat trailing down his temple. "Oh dear," I said, leaning up and wiping away the sweat before putting the back of my hand to his forehead. "Did you catch a cold?"

He cleared his throat and before he could respond, he let one rip.

I sucked my lips into my mouth and clamped down on them. "The bathroom's over there. Feel free to destroy the toilet." He took off before I could finish. I wasn't sure if the red on his neck and face was due to embarrassment or warmth. Whatever it was, I enjoyed it too much.

He slammed the door behind him, and the second he sat on the toilet, I heard all the god-awful sounds echo through the bowl and greet me down the hall. My belly ached like I'd done a good ab workout, and I could hardly hold myself up as I crawled my way to the bathroom.

"Are you—are you alright?" I wheezed out, trying to catch my breath between hyper, uncontrollable laughter. "Do you need help?"

"With taking a shit? Yes, Sophia, please," Cupid growled out, his voice strained, as more farts and plops of poop greeted me. The laxative didn't fail me. "Oh, I'm going to kill you."

"Take this as revenge for breaking into my house," I said while bent over, hysterically laughing, and forced to clench my legs so I didn't piss myself. I slid down the wall until I was curled up and shaking with silent laughter and streams of tears. "I'm so sorry, Cupid," I said when I finally calmed down a little. When he farted again, I went back to laughing. Sirus curled up between the bathroom door and me, just observing as I cackled, and Cupid groaned.

Eventually, he flushed, washed his hands, and exited with shaky legs.

"Oh, Cupid!" I cried out in disbelief at the smell that greeted me. "That's foul."

"I'll show you foul." Before I could even register his words, he had effortlessly lifted me to my feet and shoved me straight into the bathroom.

"NO!"

He slammed the door shut, leaving me entrapped in the bathroom with the horrible stench of feces that wafted through the bathroom and assaulted all my senses.

"MY EYES ARE BURNING! LET ME OUT!" I cried, violently tugging at the door as the odor closed in on me, making me gag and cough. "My God, I can taste it! I'm dying, Cupid. I'm so sorry, just let me out!" I pleaded, tugging my shirt over my mouth.

Over my loud protests, I could hear his loud, booming laughter occupy all corners of this house. Finally, he opened the door and I stumbled out, slamming the door shut.

"That's disgusting," I snapped, putting distance between the door and me while trying to catch my breath and fresh air. I glared at a bent-over Cupid, who continued to laugh. "I'll get you back."

"No," he said, shaking his head and straightening with that massive grin on his face that rewarded me with the pleasant sight of his teeth. "We're even now."

"Even," I scoffed. "You wish we were even."

"For your date tomorrow," he said with a soft chuckle, pulling out a piece of paper and tucking in into my hand. "Have fun." He still looked uncomfortable and I could only imagine the adventure his stomach must be on right now.

With a small smile, I watched his retreating back as he exited through the front.

Maybe the best way to describe him would be 'the life of the party.'

7

Hot Daddy?

The soft breeze and the smell of freshly mowed grass did nothing to ease my nerves as my Uber drove me to my date. After having several dates in the twenty-six years of being alive, I figured I'd have my sweating under control, but my body proved me wrong.

Sneaking a quick peek at the driver, I rolled the window down a little more and adjusted my arms, so they weren't tightly sealed against my body. Air flowed through the gap, cooling me off and filling the car with the scent of my strawberry deodorant.

"Haha," I said awkwardly, while peeking a glance at my unamused driver. Sweat started to form above my lips from embarrassment. "Seems like someone's selling fresh strawberries." The sweating doubled now due to the rare condition known as stupidity.

He briefly glanced at me but didn't comment. He should be grateful it smelt like strawberries and not body odor. If that were the case, I would have thrown myself out the moving vehicle and waited for oncoming traffic to crush me.

Eventually, he pulled up to my destination, and I instantly groaned.

"An elementary school?" I whispered under my breath while exiting the car. I leaned down to wave goodbye to the driver, but he sped off before I could even lift my arm. Someone was not in a good mood, but I gave him five stars anyways. We all have those days.

Turning back to my nightmare, I eyed the school with disdain.

From the looks of it, the school had been dismissed a while ago, but considering my date was at 4 o'clock, I know I'm not late. My date must be done for the day. Walking into the school and towards the office, I wondered who Cupid had set me up with this time. Maybe the secretary, or the principal, or maybe even a hot teacher. Yum. I'd be more than happy for him to teach me a thing or two.

Walking down the colorful hallway washed me with nostalgia. The walls were painted bright and vibrant with pathetic drawings that made me crack a smile at its innocence. Some of those kids will grow up to be artists one day, and others will hesitate to draw a simple stick figure in front of others, starting with, 'I'm not an artist, so please don't laugh'.

For a moment, I found myself getting sidetracked. Stopping at a bulletin board, I took in the scribbled writing that spoke of their dreams and aspiration.

When I grow up, I want to be a dad!

Biting my lips to hold in a giggle, I shook my head and continued walking. Pure innocence. I missed being young.

When I walked into the office, a plump woman with a scowl on her face that looked close to permanent greeted me. Why on Earth was she hired to work at an elementary school with a face like that? I was sure she traumatized students.

"Hey," I said, beelining towards the only staff in the front of the office. Before I could continue, something hard bounced off my back. "Hey!" I spun around and pinned the stupid child with a glare. "Watch it."

"Watch it," he mocked, tilting his head side to side like a bobblehead. His untamed hair looked like it was in knots as he tugged at it with one hand. The other hand held a tennis ball. "What are you going to do about it, fat lady?"

"You insolent little child," I mumbled and chose to ignore his fat-shaming insult before turning back to the bored lady. "I'm here for Noel King."

"What's your name?" she asked in a monotone voice that made me feel like I was at a prison, waiting to meet my foolish husband who managed to get himself incarcerated. Well, still better than having no husband at all.

"Sofia Santos," I answered.

"Great. Have the kid behind you," she said without even lifting her eyes to glance at me.

A child. I was going on a date with a child. No, I was going to prison. I wondered what the equivalent of dropping the soap was for a women's prison.

I slowly turned on my feet, ready to pick out which kid was mine but paused. My caught sight of the angled photo frame on her desk. I guess she was capable of smiling and loving. She stood with one arm wrapped around her husband's back while he kissed her temple and her four children beamed at the camera.

If she's capable of finding someone to love her, attitude and all, there must be someone out there to love me, imperfection and all.

Shaking away my longing, depressing thoughts, I turned to the children behind me and felt my heart drop to the pit of my stomach. There wasn't an abundance of children as I had thought from all the noise and ruckus I had heard. There was only one child, and he happened to be the kid who threw his ball at me.

The look of horror melted away, and I plastered the fakest smile I could muster. "Look's like your mine for the day, kid," I said in a sickly-sweet voice. He aimed his ball for my face, but I snatched it out of his small fist before he got the chance to assault me.

"I'm not going anywhere with you," he argued, crossing his little arms and slumping into the chair. I could have sworn I heard the secretary cackle softly behind me. "Give me back my ball."

"Oh, you're coming with me," I said, starting to walk away. "You're going to come because if you don't, Santa isn't going to give you that…thing you've been asking for." That was dumb. Of all threats I could have used, I used Santa, who wasn't going to grace us with his presence for another eleven months.

"I don't care about Santa," the brat argued, his voice getting closer as he caught up to me. "I don't care about anyone."

"Sure, you do," I argued. "You care about your mom."

"I don't have a mom," he retorted smugly, as if not having a mom was an accomplishment.

My heart stilled in my chest for a moment, and I found my attitude melting into a puddle of nothingness. I almost opened my mouth to apologize but thought better of it.

"What do you want to eat?" I asked. "I'll shower you with candy and cookies and soft drinks all you want."

His eyebrows furrowed inwards, and he squinted his eyes, looking at me like I offered to feed him roadkill. "Daddy only allows me to have that on the weekend," he said. "He says it's bad for me."

"Of course, it's bad for you but having it now and again isn't going to kill you. Just look at me. I'm still alive."

He looked at me. His hazel eyes scanned my face as if looking for something specific, and I squirmed away, intimidated by this six-year-old who seemed to know exactly what to look for. "Your dark circles say you're about to die." This six-year-old was about to die if he kept opening his big mouth.

Pursing my lips, I focused on calling the Uber, and he took that opportunity to snatch his ball back.

"You have a big head," he said offhandedly while bouncing the ball.

"You're rude."

"Daddy always said be honest, even if it hurts people's feelings."

"Your daddy's rude too."

"My daddy's great," he argued defensively, aiming the ball at my head and threw it. I caught it before it could do damage and tossed it back at him after tucking away my phone. "He said I'm going to be the greatest tennis player of all time."

"You like tennis?" I asked, raising an unconvinced eyebrow.

"No."

"So, your name," I started, tossing his ball back. "Is it Noel as in Christmas?"

He frowned. "No, it's Noel as in my name, dummy." He threw the ball with more force, once more aiming at my face.

"Smartypants, Noel means Christmas," I explained, tossing his ball back.

"My birthday's on Christmas," he stated with a wide, cocky grin that could convince anyone that he chose the day he would be born.

I smirked. "Must suck to get birthday and Christmas gifts combined."

The words didn't process for a moment but when they did, his eyes widened, and he denied it. "NO! I get lots and lots and lots of gifts. You wish you have that many gifts!" He may be denying it now, but his father was going to have one tough Christmas this year.

While we tossed the ball back and forth, I observed the devious child who couldn't look innocent if he tried. I think it was the hair that instantly gave him away, or maybe it was that jagged smile he gave, showing his lack of front teeth. Whatever it may be, his looks screamed Satan.

When the Uber pulled up, we both got in. "Tell her where you want to go," I told Noel.

"The library!" he said without batting an eye.

She glanced at me in the rear-view mirror, and I nodded, turning to my phone to reroute from my original destination, which was my place. "So, you're saying you're a smart boy, huh?"

"The smartest," he bragged. "My brain is so, so, so big, it'll explode out of my head." He made a 'kapow' sound, throwing his arms around and flinging back into the seat, showing an example of a bomb going off.

"What's nine plus ten?" I tested. My smile grew until it stretched from ear to ear in amusement, watching this little boy act out his imagination.

He took a moment to count on his fingers, whispering numbers to himself and resetting when he messed up. When he settled on a number, he gave me a satisfied grin and confidently said, "Nineteen."

"Wrong, it's twenty-one. I thought you said you were the smartest?" I teased, ruffling his messy hair. "Do you ever comb this nest? I think…" I trailed off, leaning close and picking apart his curls. "I think I see a baby bird."

He swatted my hand away, giving me a glare that looked adorable now but with age and practice, I was sure his glare would burn through skin. "Daddy tries to, but it hurts too much, so I always run away," he said honestly after his eyes were done silently threatening me. He swung his legs back and forth, making a lot of noise by hitting the driver's seat and the back of his seat.

"Cut that out. You're hurting the driver," I said sternly, giving him my best wide eye and furrowed eyebrow look that made his nose wrinkle.

He peered around the driver's seat, and when he saw the driver, he let up. "She's pretty," he whispered to me after a moment.

Leaning closer, I whispered, "Tell her. You'll make her day."

"Excuse me, ma'am," he started, leaning forward again. I firmly pressed my lips together and puffed out my cheeks to suppress laughter. This child's too old for his age. "I think you're beautiful." The innocence of his high, childlike voice only made it better.

"Thank you, handsome," the driver said with a thick accent and a soft laugh.

Noel set back with a hue of embarrassment and a smile of satisfaction. "She called me handsome," he whispered.

"Does that mean you have a girlfriend?" I whispered back.

"I think so. Do I get her flowers now?"

I threw my head back and laughed, joined by the mellow giggle of the driver. "Where did you learn this stuff, kid?"

"Daddy taught me," he said, puffing his chest out with pride. I waited for him to beat his chest too, but it never came. He admired his father with a passion, and I found myself wanting to meet his dad. If he was anything like this little man, it wouldn't be hard to fall for him. If Cupid planned on setting me up with a father, his plan was working.

She pulled up at the library. As we got out, he said, "Thank you. Bye!" and waved his small palm and tiny fingers. I don't often hang out with six-year-olds, but something tells me he's smaller than average for his age.

She glanced back with a warm, genuine smile that made the sun jealous and said, "Keep reading, handsome."

"I will!"

We waved goodbye before heading into the library, where librarians at the desk instantly greeted him. They cooed over him, and he charmed them by sweet giggles and toothy smiles. He proved me wrong with minimal effort: he could appear innocent without even lifting a finger, and he had them all wrapped around it.

"You're such a lady's man," I said, wrapping my arm around his neck and pulling him with me towards the children books. "Do you come here to read or to flirt?"

He shrugged my arm off and pinned me with a foul glare that instantly reminded me of the devil he truly was. "You're the worst wingman ever."

"Wingwoman," I mumbled and massaged my head as he took off between the shelves. I slumped down on one of the seats with a good book and let him go through picture books and children's books for the next hour and a half before he finally called quits.

Our next stop was Dollarama, only a ten-minute walk from the library. He chatted my ear off about stuff I couldn't be bothered with but pretended to be interested in. When we arrived in the budget-friendly store, he took off towards the arts and craft area.

"I want to paint," he demanded, putting his fists on his hips and looking up at the shelves that probably seemed infinitely tall to him.

So, we grabbed the colorful art supplies and stood in line.

"Do you have money?" I asked him after feeling around my pockets. "I forgot my wallet at home."

His eyebrows drew inwards, and he planted his fists on his hips again, staring up at me thoughtfully. "Do they accept compliments?"

he asked after a moment of deep thinking that made Aristotle look like an amateur.

"We can try."

After the man had scanned all our items and put them into the plastic bag that made sea creatures wince, he rang up the price. Noel nudged me.

"Pick me up," he demanded. Putting my hands under his pits, I lifted him, levelling him with the cashier. After a moment of both of them just staring at each other, Noel said, "Put me down. I can't compliment a baseball fan." He said that in reference to the baseball sticker on the cashier's uniform.

The cashier's lips quirked up, and when I put Noel on the floor, he leaned over the counter and said, "Baseball is the best sport out there, little man."

"Nu-uh," Noel disagreed while I paid. "Watching movies is a better sport, and it isn't even a sport."

The cashier and I shared a laugh. After he gave me my bag and the bill, Noel and I headed out to grab food from his choice of a fast-food restaurant before we settled at my place. I allowed Noel to set up the supplies while I headed to the kitchen to make our food look a little presentable and less sloppy. I filled both our cups with coke. Well, I filled my cup with coke and his with coke and water.

"You didn't even wait for me," I said with a frown, joining him at the table.

"You snooze, you lose," he said simply, continuing to finger paint.

I followed his lead and allowed him to give me directives on what to draw. Occasionally, he'd glance over to see how far I had gotten and then purposely sabotage it, followed by a sheepish grin that made me instantly forgive him. He knew how to play the game, I had to give him that.

The sun continued to beat down on us while I played soft music and allowed for us to just paint in occasional silence that Noel didn't allow to stretch on for too long. Over the blabber of his one-sided conversation, the scent of crisp jasmine, and the raw sight of my past hobby, I felt a small void being filled in my chest. The void had been suppressed and ignored for so long that when I finally acknowledged it and allowed the bandage to unravel and show the longing in my chest, my body physically reacted. Moister collected in the corner of my eyes, but I forcefully blinked them away, making my eyes ache and my head pound. Why I allowed a man to ruin me the way he had was an answer I'd never find, but if there was one thing I did know, it was that I'd never make that mistake again.

Noel hit the nail on the head of resurfacing old memories by simply walking down school halls and finger painting. Or maybe Cupid deserved all the credit.

As I swirled the cool paint around my finger, I wondered how I could let such a beautiful outlet just slip through my fingers. The calm I had been yearning for years had arrived and with it came peace. This form of outlet and finally unplugging from the brainwashing electrical devices made me feel alive again.

Noel jumped around once he finished his painting while I continued to paint on another canvas, this time using a brush and recalling the techniques I had practiced over the years. By the time I set my art to dry, Noel had passed out on the grass and the sun had taken on a warm golden hue as it began to set.

Leaning back into my seat, I pulled my knees to my chest and drank in what I'd been neglecting for years. Children lingering in their driveways, playing with chalk or blowing bubbles. The sound of children's laughter and squeals as they rode up and down the streets with their scooter or bicycles, especially now that the weather cooled down. Parents walked just a little bit behind their children as they leisurely walked towards the park. I couldn't recall the last time I took a moment to just take in a normal scene like this. Being holed up in the house was worse than I imaged.

A man strolled up my driveway, and I watched with a small smile as Cupid made a pitstop for Noel. He leaned down and grabbed Noel's arm. Gluing his first two fingers against Noel's wrist, he waited a moment before nodding his head and getting to his feet.

"Cupid, I don't know what type of woman you take me for, but I am not a child predator," I greeted when he sat down beside me in the very spot he sat in yesterday. "And say I was, as Cupid, you shouldn't be endorsing it."

"I know you're not a child predator, and we would never endorse something like that," he said, stretching his long legs out and crossing one ankle over the other while folding his hands behind his head. "But I needed a babysitter for the day. The kid's a handful."

"Tell me about it," I agreed as we both gazed at the knocked-out child. "But he was fun. How do you know him?"

"N-nephew." Cupid coughed and grabbed his neck. "Sorry."

I nudged him. "You should set me up with his dad."

Cupid's eyebrows pulled together, but he didn't look at me. "Yeah?"

"Yeah," I said, redirecting my gaze. "His dad sounds like fun. You might just have succeeded in making me fall in love."

"Trust me when I say his dad's terrible," Cupid said, rising to his feet. "You'd never be compatible with that man."

"Wait!" I stood up and grabbed his elbow as he was about to leave. "A favor for a favor. I babysat for you, so now you have to come to my parents' house with me tomorrow."

"What?"

"My mom invited me for dinner a few days ago, and I was hoping you'd send me on a real date so I could drag him to my family dinner, but so far, all I got was an elderly man, a woman, and a child, none of which will do," I explained.

"Just go alone," he said, shaking off my grip. "I don't have time for dates."

"It's not a date," I clarified, although my ears burned slightly at the mention of it. "I just want to introduce a boy to my family so I can get a little spotlight at dinner, instead of my oh-so-perfect sister." I batter my eyes and intertwined my fingers, positioning them under my chin. "Please, Cupid."

Cupid gazed down at me with an unknown glint in his eyes. He scratched the back of his head and, for a moment, didn't say anything. We just stared at each other, as we often did when he raked his brain for letters to form words, followed by sentences. His stare didn't bother me as most did.

"Come on, you owe me," I pleaded. The small voice in the back of my head said to drop it but a greater part of me couldn't; I didn't think I could bear it if he rejected me.

"Alright," he said at last, letting his arms drop with a sigh. "What time should I pick you up?"

"Thank you! Whatever time is fit for you. Dinner is at seven, but it'll take half an hour to get there." I didn't want to tell him I wanted to go earlier, especially after I pressured him to come.

He patted the top of my head as if I was a child. "See you then."

"Wait!" I called out again when he turned to leave. He paused and glance back at me without a hint of irritation or impatience as I predicted. "What type of love was this?"

"Philautia love. It's the love of the self that can be abused and lead to narcissism, but when done correctly, it leans towards self-care and looking after one's self in terms of mind and body. If there's one thing we should always remember, it's that we are incapable of loving others when we are unable to love ourselves first. It allows others to step all over us when we don't know our worth," he explained in a soothing, gentle tone and a gaze so tender, my stomach pooled with warmth and my whole body sighed.

After another second, he strode down the stairs and onto the grass, where he effortlessly picked up a snoozing Noel and held him close, ready to take him back to his father who I desperately hoped Cupid would set me up with in the near future.

After they disappeared, I packed up everything and headed inside. I made a beeline for the attic and started going through my old stuff until I came across gold: my old artwork. I spent hours just flipping through everything with tears in my eyes and a small smile.

The longer I stared at what I had abandoned, the less fond I became of Thor again. During the time we had dated, he often got upset at the faintest scent of paint and rambled on and on about an oncoming headache that never came. To protect myself from him lashing out of me, I slowly distanced myself from my pride and joy.

Flipping to an empty page on one of my hundreds of sketch books, I found a pencil and allowed myself to be carried away by the soft strokes of the led and the familiar sound of pencil against paper.

8

Family or Foe

Saturday, January 23

The burning desire to impress my parents growing up never dimmed. Till this day, I still compete with my sister for their attention. Whether it was making a bigger sandcastle than my sister or outdoing her with perfect grades, it didn't matter as long as I came up on top, but there was one problem: I never came up on top. If I made a castle that touched the clouds, she made a castle that reached the stars. If I brought home an 'A', she brought home an 'A+' and then some.

Maybe it wouldn't be so bad if it were a healthy competition, but it wasn't. It was sibling rivalry and only the best woman won. We always butted heads to get ahead, and she never took a single loss, which only led me to make poor decisions. Exhibit A: I bought a house after she announced her pregnancy just to outdo her. I couldn't forget that day if I bashed my head against the wall a million times.

'I have some news,' Elena announced on Christmas, clapping her hands to gather our attention. The air still rang with laughter

and happiness after we all exchanged gifts and settled with our drinks.

'Spit it out,' I demanded when her silence stretched for too long, making me shift forward, practically sliding off the edge of my seat. I gritted my teeth together as I waited for her to slap us with grand news that would only push me further down the ladder of failure in my parents' eyes.

Elena shot me a dirty look before continuing. 'Well, this has been a long time coming,' she started, only to pause again and find her husband's hand. He gave her a reassuring squeeze, and my stomach dropped. Mom started squealing, knowing exactly where this was heading. 'I'm pregnant!' The room exploded with praise while my insides exploded with ire.

'I bought a house,' I blurted before I could gain control over my mouth. All the sizzle of raising excitement came to a halt and all eyes turned to me. 'Yeah, I signed the papers a few days ago. I'm officially a house owner,' I said weakly, unable to find the enthusiasm just moments ago. Everyone stared at me in disbelief.

'But I'm pregnant,' Elena drawled out after a moment of stunned silence. Of course, everyone was stunned. 'Mom, Dad, you're having grandchildren!' and just like that, the attention shifted back to her, and my lie was for nothing. The lie that needed to be followed up with.

I ended up going out after New Year's to buy a house so I could stick to my lie. On the bright side, I finally purchased a house I'd been saving up for.

The memory brought a bitter taste in my mouth that I tried to swallow but nearly chocked on. Pushing the memory back into its respective corner with thoughts of rainbows and sunshine to conceal it, I finished applying the last touch of my makeup just in time for someone to ring the doorbell.

Not just someone. Not just anyone. No, this is a special man. This man is going to pretend to be my boyfriend for the night.

"COMING!" I yelled. Rushing down the stairs, I grabbed the pie off the stovetop, near the crate of tangerines. Thor made a special delivery to my house this morning and left them at my door with a note.

Sorry I couldn't wait around. I'm running late for work, but someone was selling these near my house and they were too sweet to pass up. I know just how much you love them. Have a good day, Sophia.

The second I bit into the sweet, heavenly fruit, my heart softened towards him. What a gentleman.

With a small smile, I turned off all the lights and threw open the door to greet Cupid with a bit too much zeal. "Hey," I said breathlessly as I slid into my flats.

He took the pie from my hand, his warm fingers brushing mine for only a second. "Let's go. We're going to be late."

"It's only six. What's the rush?" I asked, closing the door behind me and locking it, before following him down the stairs and to his sleek car. "Wow," I said, stunned. "Being Cupid must pay nice, huh?"

His lips tugged up, and he withheld his response until we were both in the car and buckled in. "Being Cupid is rewarding in many ways," he said and started ticking them off. "Easy lay, nice pay, and my say."

"Wrong. You have rules," I reminded.

"That I don't follow," he countered, "which means I have my own say." He rolled down both our windows an inch and turned the radio on. "The pie smells great, by the way."

I breathed in the warm smell of caramelized sugar, cinnamon, and sweet apples that wafted around us. It was a scent I could get lost in for hours and by far the most addictive thing I've come across in life.

"Although, I won't be trying it," he said with a small frown overtaking his lips. "I don't think I can risk diarrhea again."

"No, no, no," I said, my whole face lifting with humor and a small giggle spilling past my lips. "I promise I didn't do anything."

"Yeah, okay," he said sarcastically.

We filled the remainder of the drive with light banter and music. I had to admit, I appreciated Cupid's car and his driving. The exhaust of the car was slightly above the average purr of most cars. The sound used to irritate me to my core, especially the deafening ones that shook the road, but I'd found a small appreciation for them after my eldest brother managed to ingrain the sound of rumbling exhaust into my mind as the sound of beauty and grace. Although, that doesn't mean it makes me less angry when I'm startled awake by a loud car. His driving, on the other hand, managed to be both reckless and careful.

"You're gonna get yourself killed one day," I said when we finally pulled up at my parent's house.

"I'm a safe driver," Cupid argued as we both exited.

I scoffed and led him up the marbled driveway that glistened under the sun. "Safe driver? You were going twenty above the speed limit on the freeway and jumping lanes."

"Jumping lanes? Hardly," he defended. "There were just a few slow drivers I needed to pass."

"They were going the speed limit. Okay, ready?" I laid my hand on the steel doorknob. "Don't feel offended if they don't like you. You just have that vibe."

"Yeah?" he asked, raising a challenging eyebrow. "If I can charm them, you owe me."

"Alright, Mr. Perfect, challenge accepted." Although I sounded confident and cocky, my stomach was doing all sorts of flips. Pushing the door open, the blasting AC and homecooked food greeted us.

Before we could step any farther, my twin brothers came crashing out of one of the living rooms into the living room we were in, one on top of the other as they wrestled.

"SAY MERCY!" Quinn screamed when he got Wade in a headlock. "Say it!"

"Ahh," I said, breathing in deeply while taking off my flats. "Home."

"Should I pull them apart?" Cupid asked and watched them through worried eyes as they rolled around, screaming profanities and throwing blind punches.

"Nah, let's go meet my grandma," I said, grabbing his forearm and tugging him along with me. When he fell into step, I let him go and directed us into the living room that the twins rolled out of, also known as the family room.

Mom never liked us hanging out in the living room. She said it must always look presentable for when guests dropped by the house. We were too much of pigs to hang out in there and leave it in a tidy position. Lucky for her, we didn't like that room anyways. Far too impersonal and elegantly decorated for our taste.

"Lola!" I greeted my grandma the second I stepped into the room, partially out of respect but mainly because she was the apple of my eyes. That woman never saw a thing wrong with me and never failed to defend me when my parents compared me to Elena. Hell, I even loved her after she scarred me at the ripe age of three when she popped her false teeth out and laughed wickedly. Mom got mad because I pissed myself.

"You're late," she scolded, but her face told a different story. Her eyes lit up with warmth and happiness, and her lips stretched up to show her perfect row of false teeth.

"I know, I'm sorry," I apologized. I laid the apple pie down on the coffee table before leaning down to hug the tiny woman who deserved nothing but peace and bliss in her life. For a woman her age, she sure did give bone-crushing hugs. I wouldn't have it any other way.

"Soap!" my little niece, Lilly, cried out, running towards me. I pulled away from Grandma just in time to catch Lilly in my arms.

"How are you, baby?" I asked, tickling her chin. She rewarded me with a giggle, showing her tiny teeth. She planted a wet kiss on my cheek, and I let her down to continue playing but Cupid momentarily stopped her to give her a lollipop he drew out of his pocket, along with a playful wink. She happily accepted before going on her way to show her dad.

I refocused my attention on Grandma and found her shooting daggers at me. "What, old woman?" I asked, crossing my arms.

She tilted her head towards Cupid.

"Oh," I said flatly, looking at Cupid, who had a small smile on his face. "This is my boyfriend." The words taste odd in my mouth. I hadn't ever called someone that in such a long time that it felt foreign. "That's Cu—"

"I'm Lyco," Cupid cut in, taking a step forward and standing so close that our arms brushed against each other.

Lyco? He had a name. I didn't know why I never considered anything past Cupid, but it made sense since he wasn't Cupid himself.

He extended his bear-like hands to grasp my grandma's small, fragile ones in his in a gentle grip. He got down one knee, making himself eye to eye with her. "It's nice to meet you, Lola."

Grandma's annoyance melted away, leaving only the look of glistering love in her eyes and parted lips as she stared at Cupid. Reaching her free hand forward, she placed her soft and wrinkly hand on top of his head.

"I see you're a good man, Lyco," Grandma said after a moment. Her hand slid down to his cheeks, and she whispered, "Treat my girl right."

The moment entrapped something so raw, so pure that even I became entranced by the instant connection made between the most important woman in my life and the man who needed me to fall in love so he could keep his job.

Cupid seemed just as caught up in the moment as they gazed into each other's eyes as if communicating some sort of message I couldn't read. Or maybe they were falling in love. I hope not because then my grandma found love for the second time and I couldn't even find it the first time.

At last, I cleared my throat and said, "He's not that good of a man, Lola."

The intense gaze and cursed spell broke, forcing them to turn their attention to me. "That's how I know he's a great man. You'd never refer to a horrible man as such." Grandma detached herself from Cupid. "Nor would you bring him home if that was the truth."

Pursing my lips, I started walking away. "I'll let you believe that, Lola, only because I love you."

"Oh, dear girl, nothing gets passed me," she called as Cupid and I turned to the other men in the room.

"That's my dad," I said, pointing to the small man practically sunken in the wooden rocking chair. How he managed to have three six-foot-tall boys was beyond me. "That's my eldest brother, Kai, and that's my brother-in-law, Malcolm. Both are married, so keep your hands to yourself." I whispered the last part and got an amused smirk from Cupid.

He dipped his head down and his lips brushed against my ear. "I can show you tonight just how much I prefer women over men," he whispered while running his hand down my back and stopping right on my bum. It lingered for only a second before he stepped away, leaving me gaping at his back and my insides a scrambled mess. The alarm screeched inside my body, and in turn, my body responded with tingles of appreciation. I frantically looked around, hoping no one saw. Thankfully, no one did.

Cupid busied himself greeting everyone while I shook off his comment and stepped away from him, in the direction of my detached father.

"How's everything?" I asked cheerfully, wanting nothing more than to brighten his mood with my presence. Dreams were hard to let go of and this happened to be one of them. I leaned down to embrace him and he returned it with an air hug of his own, one I'd become so familiar with that I'd forced myself to find comfort in it.

"I'm still listening to your mother's nagging all day," he said, his voice void of all emotion. He settled his gaze on the television again, and I wondered if he even saw me. The only thing that will motivate him to get out of his chair is dinner and sleep. The house could be burning down and he'd continue to watch the Kotex Pad advertisement as long as it played on television.

"Oh, it's only because she loves you," I said, picking up his empty beer bottle and getting to my feet. "You should really lay off the drinks, though. You're far too old to be drinking so much, and liver cancer will knock on the door soon."

"Don't turn into your mother and sister. I hear it enough," he scolded, effectively making me shut up.

"Okay," I said meekly, putting the beer bottle back down. I turned around, ready to escape the suffocating living room but stopped short when I made eye contact with Cupid. That nosy man. The intensity of his gaze told me everything I needed to know. Prickles of anger danced up my arm and neck at him invading such a vulnerable moment with my father. Even though I tried to keep my voice low and actions shielded, I had no doubt he observed it all.

Before I got the chance to tell him off for snooping, the twins came rolling into the living room, bringing in a blasting wave of energy.

"ATTACK!" they screamed, and not a second later, they both jumped straight onto Cupids back. All three of them went crashing down, and the remainder of us winced.

"You idiots!" I snapped, stomping over to them and grabbing them by the ear. Yanking hard, I managed to get them to scramble off my fake date. The date I was doing a terrible job convincing everyone of with my snide remakes. "Don't you have an ounce of decency? Can you not be embarrassing for one night?"

"It's still day," Wade argued after they both swatted my hands away and slapped the back of my head with heavy hands.

"Ow!" I jabbed my elbows into their ribs, trying to pry them off me as they closed in on me, messing up my hair and tickling my side. "KAI! GET THEM OFF!" I screamed between giggles and shallow gasps. It was the only warning they got before they were torn away from me, taking a few strands of my hair in the process, and nearly stumbled halfway across the room.

"We're only messing with our little sister," Quinn said with a pout when Kai reprimanded them.

"These are my other dumb brothers, Quinn and Wade," I introduced, replicating Grandma's earlier stare and threw daggers at them. It never failed to amaze me how these idiots managed to find two wonderful women while I continued to struggle.

"We're the older, mature ones," Wade said, making himself comfortable. He leaned against the wall with one foot propped against the wall and schooled his expression. Just like that, they managed to suck the air dry of humor and fun, leaving it hanging heavy with unpredictability.

"Older by ten months," I interfered, grabbing my apple pie, "which makes me the youngest."

"Who are you?" Quinn asked, his lips tugging downwards, only adding to the hard expression that always unsettled me growing up. With both of them on either end, the tension carried over the whole room, blanketing us all. Even Dad noticed.

"He's my boyfriend," I introduced as Mom and Elena finally joined us. "Cup—uh, Lyco, this is my mom and my sister, Elena."

Elena stepped forward and outstretched her hand with a kind smile. "How much did Sophia pay you?" she asked when they pulled away.

"She said she'll calculate based on my behavior," Cupid answered. He shook my mom's hand with a charming, boyish smile that made me roll my eyes.

"Act yourself and I'll pay you double," Elena said, her smile widening. She threw me a quick wink and not-so-quietly whispered, "I'll save your bank account."

"I don't need saving, thank you very much," I said stiffly, turning away from her, but Cupid reached out as fast as lightning and wrapped his arm around my neck, pulling me close.

"In that case, may I mention just how foul her breath can be sometimes?"

"Oh, please, do tell," Elena said, lightly touching his elbow and redirecting him towards the couch. Quinn and Wade still weren't having any of it, which prompted them to follow me into the kitchen.

Quinn cleared his throat and Wade raised an eyebrow, both of them crossing their arms and widening their stance. As identical twins, it was hard to tell them apart at times, and right now happened to be one of them. When they were young, they'd throw a fit if Mom tried to dress them the same but as they grew older, it seemed they actually liked it. Occasionally, they'd show up dressed the exact same, making us play the guessing game. Of course, growing up with them gave us an obvious advantage and we'd figure it out in a minute flat, but it still took a little squinting, for me, at least. Mom seemed to know exactly who was who without even looking.

"Don't look at me like that," I growled, propping myself up on the spinning stool at the kitchen isle after placing the pie down. "You should be happy I finally brought someone home."

"If he's anything like the last guy, I'm beating both of you," Quinn warned.

"Both of you," Wade emphasized, setting me with a glare. "You suck at dating."

"Suck at it," Quinn repeated.

"Don't remind me," I said, screwing my face up at the mention of Thor. Everyone, including Dad, knew about Thor and what he did, and no one wanted to see his face again. If I ever did choose to get into a relationship with him again, my family would be the hardest to overcome. They did, after all, see what a mess I became after our breakup and how far I pushed them away when I was in the relationship. "But Lyco…" I trailed off. Do I tell my loud-mouth brothers the truth? "He's a good guy, okay? Trust me on this one."

Wade looked at Quinn and Quinn looked at Wade. They both nodded. "Validation bullshit," they said at once, saying the same thing they always did when they knew I was up to something.

Panic flared in my chest. "No! This one isn't for validation. This one is for my happiness."

"They're never going to love you. Give up," Quinn teased.

"Give up," Wade agreed.

Like you did? I wanted to ask. From what I know, Wade and Dad don't speak more than three words. They wouldn't speak to each other at all if they had it their way. Wade grew less and less fond of Dad the older he got, to the point where he didn't even consider him his father anymore. Said he never acted like a father, so why must he be treated as such?

Mom hated it and blamed Dad. Said if he had been a better father to his children, our family wouldn't be so divided. I said it was Mom. If she hadn't encouraged Dad's alcoholism by continuing to bring it into the house, maybe we'd all be alright. Elena blamed me. Said if the accident she considered my birth didn't happen, Dad wouldn't be so stressed about money and work overtime. Maybe then he'd be home a little more often.

Picking up the nearest thing, I threw the spoon at Wade, which he easily ducked.

"Shut up!" I yelled after the laughing twins as they walked away.

After recouping, I exited the suffocating kitchen and joined everyone. That only lasted a minute before the men had to set up the table and the women finished up in the kitchen and brought the food out.

At the dinner table, no topics were off-limits.

"Where did you guys meet?" Mom asked.

"He broke into my house," I answered and when everyone turned their attention to me, I nodded. "Yes, threatened to set me straight."

Cupid chuckled nonchalantly when all gazes flickered to him. "Real funny, Sugar," he said, putting a hand on my thigh and giving it a soft squeeze. "She's just too embarrassed to tell everyone how we really met. She asked a guy for his number at a bar, but he gave her a fake number, so she ended up calling me instead of him. We hit it off."

"The bar?" Elena asked, her eyebrows shooting up as Mom's furrowed with worry. Dad finished filling up his plate and headed out of the dining room, back to the living room to continue watching his show. "How often do you go?"

"Hardly," I lied. To be honest, in addition to observing the behavior of men, it was the most convenient place to meet a date, but it didn't mean I drank. My bartender, Emson, knew 'shot of Vodka' was code for a shot of chilled water. Then, I observed the man's facial expression as he watched me take a few in a row. If he got excited, I always left. Sometimes, I liked to sip it just to make them uncomfortable. "Oh, come on, don't look at me like that. I don't have an addictive personality."

"I don't know, Sophia," Elena said, tilting her head with false concern. "You do tend to make stupid mistakes."

"Thanks, Elena, I appreciate you mentioning my lack of smart decisions while I sit here with my date," I snapped, sitting a little straighter. "And for your information, I'm capable of taking care of myself and am in no need for your concern."

"You're right," my peacemaker brother, Kai, jumped in. "Elena was out of sorts, and Sophia, you are capable of making good decisions. Let's just eat, huh?"

Cupid rubbed my knee soothingly while changing the subjects.

"Mrs. Santos," Cupid called for my mother. She glanced up, her eyes bright and waiting for something to distract her from the usual dinner arguments. "This taba ng talangka is lovely. You'll have to give me the recipe."

Almost everyone's eyebrows raised as the man who clearly wasn't Filipino showed knowledge about the crab dish in front of him. It wasn't only his knowledge that surprised us but also his perfect pronunciation. Lola made a sound of approval. Mom was surprised for another reason.

"You cook? That's great!" she praised, her face filled with delight. "My boys are lazy. They order take out every night. Sophia, you found yourself a good one." She clasped her hands together, eyes still twinkling as she looked around the table. "You boys should be ashamed of yourself. Look at this smart man. You should all be more like him. And my god, his pronunciation is better than all of yours!"

Definitely not true but growing up in the western world did water down our appreciation for our own culture.

Now, maybe if they took us to the Filipinas and showed us around...

To be fair, Lola and Lolo from Mom's side migrated here when they were in their early 20s and never got a chance to go back home, so Mom was a little hesitant herself. As for Dad, he was too busy.

Quinn rolled his eyes, and Wade groaned.

"We can cook," Kai said, his lips pulled up in a smirk. "We just choose not to."

"Speak for yourself," Elena cut in. "Remember when Quinn tried making eggs? Not only did he burn them, but he managed to get them on fire too."

Quinn retorted with an embarrassing story of Elena about the time we went skiing and she ended up under the chair of the ski lift. She had to face the humiliation of not only that, but also having to stop the whole lift while everyone giggled behind their hands and watched. That story even made me wince.

I leaned close to Cupid. "How did you know that?"

"A lot of last-minute research and lots of hoping that at least one of the dishes I learned would be on the table. To be fair, it was also a stab in the dark when I complimented the dish because I can't quiet remember the image of it, but it just seemed like it. Also, lots of YouTube videos to learn pronunciation."

I bit my bottom lip and turned away him, pretending like my stomach didn't just suddenly swarm with butterflies and make me lightheaded.

From there, dinner continued with lighthearted conversation that made Mom melt into her seat and Lola grin from ear to ear.

Eventually, when all was done, Mom put me on washing duty, which I extended for as long as I could. By the time I completed the task, Elena started serving dessert and everyone settled into the living room. I joined and sat beside Cupid, who nonchalantly put an arm around my shoulder and pulled me close.

I stiffened and reflectively tried to shove him away but paused. Cupid was doing me a favor by trying to make up for the lost timing of trying to convince my parents that I, their lonely daughter, had settled into a committed relationship. It took a moment to lose the stiffness but when I did, I softened in his hold and leaned against him.

"So, do you guys wrestle?"

I glanced up and saw Cupid looking at my brothers, who were both busy insulting each other and eating dessert. They both looked at each other for a moment, as if wondering *is this baboon talking to us?* They looked back at him and after a small pause, Wade said, "Yeah."

"Quinn, you should work on your Nelson hold. There's too much wiggle space when you did it on Wade. Here, let me show you." I winced as I watched him get up.

Quinn put his plate down, and both he and Wade shared a smile that conveyed something terrible.

"Lyco, maybe you should—"

"Don't worry," he said, brushing me off.

Well, I tried to warn him.

They moved to the opening of the living room so not to break or damage anything. Elena shouted a warning neither of them payed any heed to.

They both got in a starting stance and…

Hm, maybe I should have warned Quinn instead.

It was over before it started and Quinn was on the floor, groaning and yelling censored profanities like 'frick' and 'goshdamn it' that Elena still wasn't fond of. She covered Lilly's ears while glaring at them both. But still, when he rose, there was newfound respect in his eyes.

Wade pushed through and challenged Cupid, only to be dropped in a matter of seconds as well. I turned away as Cupid started showing them certain angles and different positions and holds and throws and strikes that I couldn't be bothered with. I turned my focus to playing catch with Lilly.

At some point during the night of interrogation, teasing, and arguments, Elena called for everyone's attention. "I have good news," she started, prompting me to roll my eyes. Thankfully, she didn't see.

"Spit it out," Quinn demanded impatiently.

She shot him a glare before setting her tender gaze on my parents. Of course, the announcement had no place for anyone in this room but my parents. I braced myself for her to rub in her next milestone, so I could be pushed down one more step in my ladder of shame. "I got a promotion at work!"

Before she finished, the room already began to ring with congratulations and praise, but I couldn't find it in me to even open my mouth. Of course, she got a damn promotion. I've been working years for a promotion, only to continue to sit at the same cubical for years, and she got a promotion just a month after I shared my struggle with her and Mom.

"Aren't you happy, Sophia?" Elena asked, taking notice in my lack of enthusiasm. I didn't realize until she called for my attention, but I had pressed myself so close into Cupid's side, I was surprised he didn't ask me to ease up or I'd bruise him.

"Of course," I said, getting to my feet. "You got that promotion you were working so hard for." No one missed the sarcasm in my voice. "I have a few things to do tomorrow and have an early start, so I'm gonna head out. I'll see you soon."

I got to my feet, kissed Lola, Mom, and Dad and then headed out without a glance back at my siblings. Why did I have to be the runt of the family? It was dark back here, hiding in the shadows of my siblings.

9

They Love Me, They Love Me Not

Saturday, January 23

The drive back to my place consisted of few words exchanged and background music. Cupid and I were too occupied with our thoughts—or maybe we were both drained—to give each other attention.

I leaned against the window and closed my eyes, allowing myself to drift off and hover between reality and dreamland. Just as sleep started to sneak into my foggy mind, the car came to a halt and the engine cut to silence.

Blinking my eyes open, I stifled a yawn and unbuckled. "Thanks for—this isn't my house." Outside the windshield, a neon sign glared at me. Cherry on Top. "Is that an…ice cream shop?"

"You owe me," Cupid said, unbuckling the seatbelt and getting out without another word.

"I owe you?" I asked in disbelief, also getting out. "For what?"

"I charmed your family, didn't I?" he asked, raising a cocky brow. I slammed the car door shut, making Cupid wince.

"Hardly," I scoffed, striding straight past him and throwing open the store's door. I didn't bother holding it open for him. Truth be told, Cupid did charm everyone in that room, twins included. By the end of the night, they had all warmed up to him, and even Dad managed to crack the briefest smile at one of his lame jokes. "Two vanilla ice creams with sprinkles and in that…uh, sprinkle cone please," I said to the cashier. Cupid hovered behind me while she typed it in.

"What makes you think I want sprinkle vanilla ice cream?" he asked, waving his card in front of me but I beat him to it and paid.

"You're just a vanilla type of person," I said, turning back to throw him a quick smirk.

"You should come over and find out just how vanilla I am."

I gasped at the suggestive tone, completely turning around to gape at him. "Cupid!" It didn't stop me from cackling. I think the cashier even let a snicker slip. I couldn't help but notice his second 'you should come over and find out' advancement but brushed it off as friendly flirting.

"What?" he asked innocently.

A few minutes later, with our ice creams in hand, we stepped outside to sit on the seats provided.

"I had fun tonight," Cupid started. "Your family is great."

"Yeah," I mumbled, tilting my head to the side.

"You don't think so?" he pried.

I side-eyed him, understanding his attempt at getting information out of me. "Yeah."

The silence stretched between us, turning our relaxed bodies into manikins as we waited for the other to crack. He did. "Tonight, I saw a struggle between you and your family," he started, leaning back into the hard metal chair.

"I don't want to talk about it." I busied myself with licking my ice cream, so I had an excuse not to talk to him, but Cupid didn't care.

"Sure, you do," he encouraged. "Let me in a little bit. Give me some perspective into your life."

He wanted perspective I didn't have. All I knew was that I occupied the spot at the bottom of the barrel, and they were better off without me. "I guess my sister and I just compete for my parents' attention. I don't know," I said lamely, hoping the answer satisfied him enough to get him off my back.

It didn't. "It seems to me you're the only one competing for the attention. She's already got it," Cupid said after finishing licking off all the sprinkles.

"Then why does she insist on showing off every opportunity she gets? Every month, it's something new with her," I grumbled, unable to hide my bitter tone that coated my entire body.

"Maybe, just maybe, she wants to share her success with her family. I might be wrong, but maybe she wants her sister to be happy for her," Cupid said. Although his words hinted at uncertainty, the look he gave me said he'd never been wrong a day in his life.

"You are wrong—ah shit, look what you made me do." In my haste of aggressively licking my ice cream, a chunk fell off, missing my leg by an inch and splatting onto the cemented ground.

Cupid held his ice cream to my mouth and with the use of my lips, I took off the tip of the ice cream and swirled it around my mouth. "When Elena announced her promotion, she asked you if you were happy for her. When you brushed her off, her whole face dropped."

"Thanks," I said, referring to the ice cream he shared. "But you're still wrong. Elena doesn't care about me. She cares about being the center of my parents' attention." The argument, even to my ears, sounded uncertain. I stole a glance at Cupid, hoping he was lying, but nothing gave him away. "And besides, she only worked for that promotion because she knew I wanted it."

"How did she know?"

"I mentioned it last month."

"Well, Sophia, it takes a lot longer than a month to work for a promotion, so I can promise you she's been working just as hard as you have to get it. She didn't do it to one-up you."

"Oh, so this is all my fault, huh?" I asked, pushing my chair away from him and refusing to make eye contact. "I'm the only one making a mess in my family. I can't do anything right."

"I'm not saying it's your fault—" I shoved aside his hand when he reached for me, feeling my blood sizzle under my skin.

"Yes, you are."

"No, I'm not," he said, his voice stern. "In this case, yes, I do think it's all in your head. Promotions take longer than a month to achieve. But I'm sure, without a doubt, that she also has a part in fueling your anger and playing dirty."

When I kept my gaze steadfastly fixed on the sky, he sighed.

"She does care about you, just like how you care about her. No matter how much you both try to hide it under persistent competition, you both love each other," Cupid said, his voice as gentle as his words now, losing the attitude. He shifted his body to face me and with one hand, shifted my chair so it was tilted towards him. I stubbornly continued to gaze at the sky. "Stop being enemies."

"I don't want to be enemies." My gaze finally drifted away from the dark sky and met his direct gaze. "I just want to be noticed."

"They do notice you, Sophia. You're not invisible." I found myself leaning forward into the comfort of his syrup words as they seeped right into me.

"You think so?" I whispered, letting my desperation for validation show.

He nodded his head. "What makes you think otherwise?"

"My mom…growing up, she used to compare me to my sister's success, and I vowed to never do that with my children, assuming I even have them," I added with a forced smile. "And my dad, I swear alcohol poisoning will be the death of him. I swear he loves it more than me."

"Sophia…" Cupid trailed off, squinting his eyes as he tried to get a better look at me. "You know they love you, right?"

"Sure," I agreed. Cupid didn't say anything, prompting me to say the words on the tip of my tongue that I tried so hard to swallow. "I mean, I'm their child. They have to love me, right? Right, Cupid?"

"The love parents have for their children is pure and hard to replicate until you have a child of your own," Cupid said wisely. "So yes, they love you with all their heart."

I leaned away from him, returning my eyes to the sky and licking my ice cream that was melting down the cone and onto my fingers.

"He's never really been a father to me," I finally admitted, more to myself than to Cupid. "Sure, he's my biological father who provided for the family and hasn't abandoned us, but it was always Mom who raised us. Dad was always off on trips for work for months on end, and when he came home, he would drown himself in alcohol before heading back to work. He was never there for much of my successes, so he's kind of a stranger to me.

"And you know," I touched Cupid's arm, just to make sure I had his full attention as I mentioned the next part. "I think it may add to my anger towards my sister. She's the second oldest, which means she and my older brother got most of the attention from Dad. He went to all their games and recitals and graduation. Hell, he was even in the hospital when she gave birth. Dad didn't even come to my house until a year after I bought it."

As I spoke, Cupid nodded along. He positioned his body towards me, his eyes gazing at mine even if I avoided his. Cupid casted a spell on me—one that made me spill all my secrets I would never dream of sharing with anyone, but something told me my secrets were safe with him.

I nibbled away on the cone, noticing that Cupid had abandoned his ice cream altogether. "I always wanted to be Daddy's little girl, but the spot's taken."

Cupid placed a warm hand on my knee. "Your dad loves you," he said in a voice just below his average tone. "You need to understand that. He just shows it differently."

"How?" I asked, far too stubborn to accept this reasoning. "I bet he forgets I even exist half the time."

"He got up to hug you. That's not something many fathers do if they don't like their children. Especially if they're as emotionally distant as you say he is. You're so wrapped up in the bad, you're overlooking the good, and that's hurting your relationship with your family," Cupid said.

For the next little while, I finished my ice cream while pondering over Cupid's intense knowledge that he shoved onto me in an attempt to get me to understand my family.

Back inside the car, I asked Cupid, "Can you drop me off at a hotel? I don't want to go home right now."

"Too lonely?" he asked, as if he read my mind.

I simply nodded. "We should exchange numbers. Easier to communicate."

Cupid didn't hesitate. "This will be easier to get in contact with you," he agreed, and we exchanged phone numbers.

When Cupid pulled up at a building in the heart of downtown, I realized I should have specified.

"I meant somewhere cheaper," I said flatly.

"I live here," Cupid informed, pulling up at the garage and scanning his card. "Just don't ask any questions when we get to my place."

"What? Why? I mean, why are we here?" I asked, bewildered. I didn't think he would actually make good on his suggestive comments from earlier.

"Because you're sad," he admitted. "And no one deserves to be alone when they're sad. It leads to terrible things."

"You take your job too seriously sometimes, you know that?" I asked in astonishment. He parked in his spot, and we both got out.

"You can never take being Cupid too seriously." He locked the car, making it beep twice and echo.

I busied myself checking out the garage, and then the elevator, followed by the hallway of the last floor. Being Cupid truly did pay well and if his car didn't show it, then his living situation sure did.

When we stopped at the last door at the end of the hall, Cupid said, "remember, no questions." He unlocked the door and pushed it open, revealing the homey feel of his condo. I didn't get much time to observe before a high-pitched voice cut into my thoughts.

"Daddy!" a voice happily greeted. Before I could process the words, a ball of messy hair flew out from behind a corner and latched onto Cupid's leg.

"I tried to get him to sleep but he refused," another familiar voice said, rounding the corner as well. "Oh, hello Sophia."

I stepped back, my mouth hanging open as I stared at all three of the people in the room. "Lubin?' I asked, my voice colored with betrayal. "Noel? As in your son?"

"Ahh," Lubin said, pursing his lips. His sharp eyes cut to Cupid. "Well, this isn't a conversation I want to be a part of. Kiss me goodbye, boy."

Noel let go of Cupid and turned to Lubin, who effortlessly picked him up. Noel planted a wet kiss on his cheek before being set down. "I'll see you tomorrow." He gave me a nod and squeezed Cupid's shoulder before exiting.

"You have a son," I said plainly, leaning back against the wall and watching as Noel tried to drag Cupid away. "And Lubin isn't actually in a senior home."

"Noel, go to your room and get in bed. I'll be there in a moment," Cupid said, untangling Noel from himself and giving him an encouraging push in the direction of his room.

Noel pouted but didn't argue. The room cleared out faster than it had been filled, leaving a rush of emotions hanging over my head. With it just being the two of us, I stared at Cupid with wide eyes, waiting for a much-needed explanation. Cupid scratched the back of his head but met my gaze head-on.

"No questions, remember?" he reminded me, closing the door and locking it. "I'll show you to the guest room. Is there anything you want to eat?"

"No, thank you," I managed to say past the haze that took over my brain.

Cupid led me past the kitchen, past the living room, and down the hall, until we stopped at the guest room. I could no longer contain the questions.

"Come on. You have to tell me a little bit," I pleaded. "You set me up on a date with your grandfather and your son. I can only assume that the woman was your sister, right? Not to mention, I went on a date with you. If I told people I went on a date with every member of a family, imagine how that must make me look."

"Well, it's a good thing you don't have to tell anyone," he stated, crossing his arms and widening his stance to look intimidating. It worked.

"Fine," I mumbled, pushing over the door and entering the room. "But this conversation isn't over." Once I was inside the room with the door closed and the light on, I took a look around.

The room lacked the life the rest of the condo had. The walls outside their room were scribbled on with markers, pens, and pencils. Maybe even some paint. Although most of the toys were tucked away in their respective spots, a few of them peaked out from under couches and past corners. Frames and pictures were decorating the wall with faces of his family. The place screamed home.

Tucking myself under the covers, I closed my eyes and reflected on the messy day I had. For some reason, finding out about Cupid's child concerned me above all. It almost hurt that he kept this from me, not that he was under any obligation to tell me anything, but he knew my life inside and out and I barely knew a thing about him.

It felt like every relationship I'd ever been in.

***

The sound of faint rustling stirred me awake. I continued to lay motionless, my eyes prying themselves open with such force that I knew it wasn't my normal time of awakening. It must still be late into the night.

Then, I felt the faintest tickle of something against my neck, making me gasp and swat at my neck. All sleep flew out the window and I jumped straight into a sitting position, turning to face the figure on my bed.

"Cupid," I hissed, clenching my chest. "What the hell are you doing?"

"Sor-sorry," he stuttered, equally as startled as he got to his feet. "Sophia, I'm so sorry."

"What were you doing?" I yelled in a whisper, holding the duvet close to my chest. The moonlight spilt into my room, allowing me a good look at his embarrassed and worried face.

"It's a really bad habit. I forgot to warn you," he said, raising an arm and scratching the back of his neck.

"What is it?" I mumbled, sitting a little higher.

"I—I…" He averted his eyes, avoiding all eye contact. "I always wake up in the middle of the night and can't fall asleep until I know everyone under my roof is alive. I tried to refrain myself from coming into your room, but I couldn't shake the thought that you…" he cleared his throat. "So, I just peeked inside, and you sleep like a dead starfish and it only scared me more, so I had to check for a pulse. I couldn't find it on your wrist and panicked, so I tried your neck."

"Why do you…" I trailed off, staring at the vulnerable man before me. Unable to stand still, he resorted to shifting on his feet, looking at anything and everything but me. "Well, alright. I'm alive. I'll see you in the morning?" I asked softly, wanting to put him out of his misery.

"Yeah." His chest deflated with relief, and he practically fled out of the room.

When the door closed behind him, the room lightened with the overpowering feeling of amazement at witnessing a part of Cupid I never thought existed. Who knew the confident, egotistical man could feel such high degree of embarrassment that put me to shame?

It took a moment to find sleep again, but I eventually did, well assured that Cupid wasn't going to let me die in my sleep tonight.

10

Sweet Poison

Sunday, January 24

Upon waking up at my usual scheduled time, the sun greeted me. Turns out, only the sun would greet me this morning.

Cupid's embarrassment from the middle of the night stretched well into the morning. It got so bad that whereas once, he was unable to maintain eye contact, now he couldn't stand in the same room as me. He sent Noel into the living room with a paper containing the usual information of my next date. He even had the nerve to write additional information about my Uber being here in five minutes. That stupid bastard.

I sent Noel back to Cupid with a note that read one word: *Coward.*

I didn't wait for the five-minute buzzer to ring. I'll get my own damn Uber. Gathering whatever leftover dignity I had, I held my head up high, pushed my shoulders back, and strode out of the place. The only sign of weakness evident on my face was the glistening tears I refuse to let fall.

Not only did I open up to him last night about my deep-rooted issues with my family, but I also found immense trust and comfort in him that was rare to me. For the short moment I had this, it tasted like a sip of crisp spring water and a breath of fresh air, only to find out it was poisoned by the same person I trusted.

Cupid showed me in less than a few words just how little I meant to him.

Just like he had no grounds for ignoring me, I had no grounds for being upset. I tried to reason with myself, tried to make my heart hurt a little less, as I told myself that I was only his project he needed to complete to maintain his job. My heart squeezed painfully, proving my reasoning to be stupid.

When I finally got home, I dragged myself into the kitchen and started on some new recipes I'd been wanting to try while Sirus made herself comfortable on the dining table and watched me.

"How many times have I told you the dining table is off-limits?" I asked while grabbing the flour.

She meowed, almost sounding like a crackled, broken laugh. She didn't move, and I didn't bother her. I just focused on making s'mores lasagna, gingerbread bars, and salted caramel cheesecake. By early evening, the kitchen was sparkling clean and my desserts waiting to be eaten.

"Do you want some?" I asked Sirus when I sat down on the floor in front of the sink with my desserts laid out in front of me.

She sniffed around before settling beside my knee. Just as I sliced into the S'mores, someone knocked on the door. I continued making perfects cuts, not wanting to talk to a salesman or a

Mormon. The door squeaked open, and I cursed myself for not locking it.

"Sophia?"

I silently continued with cutting into the gingerbread bars, this time making triangles. He silently moved around the house with grace that made ballerinas jealous. Eventually, he leaned over the aisle and hummed.

"How did I know you'd be here?" Thor asked, praising himself on remembering past knowledge.

"What do you want?" I asked, glaring down into the cheesecake while cutting them into circles.

He walked around, hiked his jeans up a little and sat down with one knee pulled to his chest. "Can I have?" he asked, reaching for the gingerbread bars.

"No." I pointed the knife at his hand, and he effectively retrieved it.

"Why are you in such a bad mood?" he asked with a soft chuckle. "I can't believe you're still cooking up a storm when you're upset."

I paused, waiting for another comment. A comment about my weight that he loved to often bring up in our relationship. He didn't.

"I am not upset." I chewed the cheesecake and swallowed, but it took more force than usual and tasted like moist dirt with sugar. My mind was too focused on one of my hands crossed over the side of my body and grabbing my love handles to care about how the food tasted.

Thor's go-to joke or insult was my lack of ability to look like Kim Kardashian. Joke's on him because this is what a real woman looks like: flab under my arm, not the perkiest bum, hair on my knuckles, and fat thighs. Not silicon booty, injected lips, and microblade eyebrows. Having all that does doesn't invalidate a woman but neither does not having it done. No matter how much Thor pushed, it was the one thing I didn't give him power over. I spent far too long loving my body for him to try and tear me down.

"You're upset," he said softly, grabbing both of my hands and getting up. "Come on, stop eating your feelings and tell me what's wrong."

When I turned my glare up to meet his kind eyes with wrinkles at the corner from smiling too often, I let my guard slip and let him hike me to my feet effortlessly. I toed the knife, sliding it to a hidden corner so he couldn't grab it if he planned on it. When he pulled me to his chest for a hug, it felt a little like a brick with all the solid muscles, and I tried to get comfortable but failed.

"Cupid and I got into a fight." Not a fight, per se, but close enough.

"You're still talking to him?" he asked gently. All my anger and resentment towards him trickled away the longer he gazed at me with an assurance of catching me when I fall.

"Yes because I believe him. Well…I did believe him. The more I think about, the stupider I look. On the last few dates, he set me up with his grandfather, sister, and six-year-old son. Maybe I am getting scammed, Thor." I couldn't stop myself if I tried. All those hours of baking and cleaning had done nothing to ease my thoughts and put things into perspective. Maybe Thor could. "And he didn't even tell me any of this. I had to find out myself last night. I feel cheated because I trusted him." The tears threatened to spill but I kept them at bay. Thor hated tears. He said it made me weak. "But to be fair, he did introduce me to them on reasonable grounds. Like I met his sister and it was to show me platonic love. I don't know, Thor."

"Say he is Cupid and it isn't a lie," Thor said, his voice soft enough to lull a wailing baby to sleep, "don't you think when he completes his job, he'll take everyone with him? You'll be back to square one. I don't know how to tell you this, Sophia, but he's only in it for himself. He needs to keep his job, and once he gets that, he'll forget all about you and move on with his life, taking his family with him."

I blinked fast and hard, begging my tears to stay hidden.

Thor pulled away and titled my chin up to look at him. "Sophia, he doesn't care about you," he whispered. His words struck my heart hard and engraved themselves there. "I'm telling you all this because I care and I don't want to see you get hurt." He wrapped an arm around my lower back and encouraged me to walk forward, which I did sloppily.

In my confused and hurt haze, we had somehow teleported from the kitchen to my bedroom and Thor was nudging me into bed. I rolled in, blinking up at him.

"His family is in on the game, too. They don't want to see him jobless." He brushed my hair out of my face when I lay down. I blinked up at him, and he gave me a sad smile. "You're so beautiful, you know that?" he asked, his smile stretching a little more.

That was all I needed to lift my spirits. "Thank you," I mumbled.

We both sat in silence for a few minutes, finding some form of comfort in each other's presence.

"Do you remember when we met?" he asked while grabbing strands of my hair, probably to braid them, as he loved to do.

That effectively made me smile. "I accidentally walked into the bathroom and there you were, using the urinal."

"You didn't run away. You just stood there and accused me of being in the woman's bathroom." We both laughed at that.

"To be fair, someone drew a skirt on the man symbol for the washroom. I really did think it was the women's washroom."

His eyes lit with humor. "You almost convinced me I was in the wrong washroom. I really thought I would get kicked out of my program if I was."

We fell into a soft silence then, and I found myself slowly starting to drift off.

"Sophia, you're a strong woman. You were then, and you are now." He leaned down and kissed my forehead. "I'll put everything away and lock up before I leave. I just want you to sleep."

My muddled, sad brain sparked with happiness, and I gave him a genuine, small smile. I caught myself before I said, 'I love you.'

11

Painful Love

Monday evening, I found myself outside my usual bar, waiting to meet my new date. Maybe this time my date would be Cupid's cousin or father or maybe even mother. Whoever it may be, they were in for a hell of a surprise, wrapped up in a sweet smile. Whoever my victim was, they were going to get a piece of my mind so that word could spread through the family and no one would be next in line to do Cupid's dirty work.

Maybe I shouldn't have come on the date at all, but I needed to get out of the house before my thoughts drowned me. I already finished all the sweets and knew if I continued to stay holed up, I'd only bake more and give myself diabetes.

Pushing open the door with more force than needed, I entered the bar and took my usual seat.

"The usual?" my favorite bartender asked.

"Yes, please."

He chuckled, and while filling up my drink, he asked, "So, who's the new guy?"

"I don't know, Em," I said. "Cupid decided to surprise me with one."

"Cupid, huh?" Emson asked, handing me my shot of chilled water. "Is that fat baby capable of running your hectic love life?"

Cupid is anything but a fat baby, I wanted to say. A handsome man suited him well, but I didn't say it because I couldn't bring myself to admit those thoughts out loud. The enemy had no right to be portrayed in such a respective manner.

"Running my love life?" I asked. "That man sucks. So far, he's set me up with an elderly man, a lesbian, and a child. We'll find out if today, he set me up with a lizard."

"I wouldn't call myself a lizard."

Emson and I both turned to the side to eye the hunk of a man before us.

"Pardon?" I asked, sitting a little straighter.

"Pardon," Emson mocked in a high-pitched voice before moving away to greet his other customers, letting his chuckle linger between the handsome man and myself like a fading cloud.

"Sophia, right?" he asked in his sexy, deep voice. He added something, but due to his low voice and the loud music, I couldn't hear anything.

"Huh?" I leaned in, squinting my eyes and staring at his lush pink lips, waiting to read what he repeated. He surprised me by also leaning in a little. Our cheeks brushed and I felt his breath against my ear when he spoke.

"I said I think I won the jackpot."

"Oh." I leaned back, hoping he couldn't see the color he painted my cheeks. Turning away, I drowned my shot of water, taking the time to come up with something funny or some form of comeback. "I didn't." Lame.

"You think so?" he asked, his vibrant green eyes light with amusement as he took his seat. "By the end of the night, you'll feel otherwise."

"Yeah?" I asked, feeling my breathing start to get shallow as he looked at me with his piercing gaze that made warmth pool in my stomach and forced me to clench my legs. I became acutely aware of every inch of my body pulsing with excitement and couldn't help but lean forward.

"Yeah." He grasped the side of my face with one hand, and we were leaning in close. Our lips met in the middle, and fireworks went off above my head.

It had been so long since I had romantic contact with someone that I savored every moment of this one. I didn't normally move this fast in relationships. In fact, by this point, I would have already been out the door due to intimidation or boredom or annoyance or fear. But he managed to keep me plastered to my seat with anticipation.

We were brought back to reality when Emson said, "Get a room."

Bright red marred my face as I pulled away and bit my bottom lip.

"Wanna get out of here?" he asked, already on his feet.

"Sure," I said. I glanced at Emson, who gave me a wink and a wide, proud smile. I took his offered hand, feeling the calluses worked up from rough, long days at work. After I jumped down, he led me out of the place by a tight grip and demanding tug. There was nothing gentle about him.

This was what I needed after the muddled mess with Cupid and Thor. I needed to clear them both from my head, and this man was capable of exactly that.

In the car ride to his place, he gripped my thigh firmly and made patterns on my knees that made me swoon. I thanked the stars for the short ride because, within minutes, we were in his room.

It may not have been the love I desired with a strong foundation and a long-term future, but it would fill the void in my chest that just kept growing.

This was going to be a fulfilling night.

***

"I feel so unfulfilled and dirty," I sobbed into the phone. "I want to scrub my body clean one hundred times and never leave my house again." It only made the void grow larger.

"Sophia? Where are you?" Cupid asked, his voice groggy with sleep but became more alert with each word.

"I'm walking home," I mumbled through my quivering lips.

"It's midnight. Get an Uber, and I'll meet you at your place."

"Okay."

"Don't hang up until—"

I hung up and shuffled the rest of the twenty-minute walk back to my place in the pelting rain that seemed to understand my pain.

My clothing stuck like a second skin against my body, wrapping me up in the comfort of the cold. My hair lay plastered to my skull and face, making it hard to see, but I walked aimlessly anyways, knowing I would find my way home eventually. Sure enough, I did.

Cupid sat on my front steps, drenched to his bones as well. My crying had quieted down during the walk back, but when I approached him, I started to shake as another round of fresh tears escaped.

He opened his arms, and I fell into them, cuddling close to his chest as I shamelessly wept under the dark clouds and soothing rain.

"I feel cheap and used. I knew this after-effect would happen, and I still choose to follow through. I feel like a terrible person," I ranted. "He kicked me out and said I wasn't of much use anymore. Granted, those weren't his exact words, but it might as well have been." I fisted my hands into his shirt as agonizing pain rippled through my chest, making it difficult to breathe. "Why would you do that to me, Cupid? Was it to get back at me for the other night?"

"No, no, no," Cupid repeated over and over and over until he found his voice again and said, "I would never do that to you. I'm so sorry, Sophia. I'm so, so sorry." He held me tighter against his warm body, wrapping me in the comfort I desired. His familiar scent soothed my headache and reminded me I wasn't alone.

"Cupid." My body shook uncontrollably from sobs. Tilting my head up, I looked into his dim, sad eyes. "What type of love is this?"

"Eros love," he whispered. "Love of the body." He didn't elaborate any more, but it was a simple reminder that the seven

Greek loves weren't always going to be painless and rewarding. To each their own.

I don't know how long we both sat there with his large, comforting arms wrapped securely around my body. We sat even after my crying dimmed into silence, but the sky never let up. It made me feel an ounce better knowing the clouds understood the sharp pain in my chest that refused to settle and the overflowing thoughts in my head that were going to make me call in sick at work for the next several days.

When I started to drift off, I felt Cupid's hesitant fingers on my neck, looking for a pulse. I allowed it. When he found it, his tense body relaxed, and I gave it another moment before I lifted my head and sat up.

Unable to meet his eyes, I got to my feet and limped to the front door. "Thanks for listening to me," I mumbled in a tone so quiet, I wasn't sure he heard. I unlocked the door and stepped inside. When I glanced back, I found Cupid still sitting on the steps with his hunched over back facing me. I wanted to say something more but had no words left, so I just closed the door, locked it, and curled up on the tiled floor, allowing myself to be lulled asleep by the sound of the tapping rain.

12

Lovesick

Tuesday, January 26

Catching a cold is one of the worst things that can happen to me. As someone who prided themselves on being independent and strong, I sure did turn into a baby when I so much as had a sniffle, but what I had now wasn't just a sniffle. No, it was a catastrophe.

"Sirus, I'm dying. Help me," I whined to my cat before falling into a coughing fit she's gotten used to. She continued to lay beside me on the kitchen floor, where I had melted into after pathetically trying to grab ingredients for soup.

After waking up in a puddle of water with my wet clothing still clinging to my body and unable to breathe through my nose, I called into work and announced that I wouldn't be coming in for the next several days because I was dying a slow, painful death.

Rebecca just laughed, wished me a speedy recovery, and hung up.

After taking a painfully long time dragging myself upstairs and nearly falling twice, I scrubbed myself clean under steaming water and changed into warm clothing. Then, I busied myself studying

Eros love, which only lasted a total of five minutes because my splinting headache only got worse.

Cupid provided Eros love. While he's well known for bringing couples together, Eros love was mainly sexual, lustful attraction. The irony of the most painful love I experienced was Cupid's love made me laugh until I couldn't see straight. And then I cussed him out.

At some point, I must have fallen asleep on the cool tiles because loud knocking awoke me.

"Coming," I yelled in a hoarse voice while crawling my way to the front door. Grabbing hold of the handle, I used it to pull myself up and braced myself for human company. Pulling open the door, I met with the sight of three sympathizing smiles.

"What are you guys doing here?" I asked and sniffled unattractively.

"Cupid figured you may be sick, so he sent us to check up on you," Alex said. "Although, he was leaning more towards heartbroken than literally being sick. Had I of followed my guts, I would have brought you soup."

"But we did bring movies and candy," Olah said. They all piled in when I opened the door wider, making room for them. Cece hung out at the door for a moment, eyeing me worriedly.

"I'm contagious," I told her with a weak smile. "I can wear a mask."

She giggled and shook her head. "I was thinking about going to the store and getting you cough syrup and whatnot."

"Yes please!" Alex called, already having taken a position in the kitchen. "Thank you, Cece!"

"No worries," Cece replied. She gave me a smile in answer to my look of gratitude and walked back out to her car, spinning her keychain around her finger. I closed the door and leaned heavily against the wall, trying to blink away the blurriness. When I finally joined Alex and Olah in the kitchen, I found that they had already started working on the soup.

"Thank you so much. I really appreciate this," I said, slumping down on the chair.

"That's what friends are for," Olah said, shooting me a wild look. "Don't say thanks. It should be expected."

"I guess so," I said with uncertainty. I could never expect this from anyone but Mom. "So, what exactly did Cupid say?"

"Well, after waking me up in the middle of the night to look after Noel and rushing out to get you, he came back drenched and covered in blood. I was actually hoping you'd be able to tell me what happened," Alex said softly, gazing at me with gentle eyes that held no blame.

"He came back bloody?" I asked. My stomach twisted up in knots and a lump formed in my throat, making it hard to ask more questions.

"It seemed like he got into a fight," Alex answered. "He wouldn't let me see his wounds, but I did see him wrapping his knuckles before I left."

Shame and guilt clawed at my throat, making me feel more suffocated than I already am.

"This is all my fault," I mumbled. Both stopped shifting around to hear me better. "I should have known better than to call a father in the middle of the night. He has his son to look after and doesn't need me disrupting him—"

"Don't," Alex said sternly. "Don't blame this on yourself. If you need Cupid, you call him. Or us. I don't have a kid to look after, so I'll be more than happy to answer midnight calls."

I nodded, saying my gratitude before continuing with the story. A few minutes later, I finished with, "I told him that this was his payback for whatever happened between us the night before and that's why he set me up with an awful man. He said he'd never do that to me. Anyways, I went inside my house and called it a night, so I don't know what's up with the blood but…"

Realization dawned on both their faces and I couldn't handle looking at them anymore.

"I'm sorry," I mumbled. "I didn't mean to get him into that kind of mess. I didn't know he'd do something like that."

Alex and Olah both walked over to me and kneeled at my side.

"Listen to me when I say no one controls Cupid's actions but himself," Alex said, putting a comforting hand on my thigh.

"No, really," Olah said. "One time a guy dumped me by asking Justin Bieber to make a Cameo breaking up with me. It was so pathetic, and I ended up hating my favorite artist for it too. The stupid idiot thought it'd lessen the blow if it came from someone I obsessed over."

I couldn't help a laugh.

"So, Cupid found my ex and drilled a good lesson into him about how to treat a woman," Olah finished. "He didn't hurt him or anything, but he did scare the ever-living shit out of him. So much so, that he came to personally break up with me and apologize too."

"He's not hot-headed all the time, nor violent, but he is protective, and it can bring out the worst in him when he sees someone hurt," Alex explained while I looked at them with wide eyes. "He probably went to your date's house to ask what happened and your date must have said something foolish to invite such violence from Cupid. Trust me when I say it didn't happen unprovoked."

"Okay," I accepted at last. "Thank you."

They returned to cooking, putting on soft music and cracking wild and nasty jokes that had me bent over laughing, wheezing, and coughing. Cece joined midway and gave me a dirty look when I asked how much it cost, before joining the other girls in cooking.

Then, we all sat together to enjoy the chicken soup and garlic bread while they went around telling stories about what happened at work. Turns out these three were the proud owners of the spa I met them at. From what I observed on my date there, it seemed successful, and they planned on making even greater improvements.

While Alex and Olah did the dishes, which I was eternally grateful for, Cece took me back to my room and gave me my medicine.

I took my medicine while she turned on the humidifier to help with congestion. I rubbed Vics on my throat while she got me a jug of warm water with drops of electrolytes. Alex informed me that the soup was covered and on the dining table and she'd be back tomorrow to check up on me.

Unable to put into words the gratitude I felt towards them, I simply said, 'thank you,' and waved goodbye. The last time someone took this much care of me was when I still lived with my parents six years ago and Mom took it upon herself to look after her daughter.

I had to ask myself if this was all an act to save Cupid. But no one would go this much out of their way for someone they don't care about, right?

Thor was wrong. He had to be wrong. These girls wouldn't leave me once Cupid completed his job. Hell, I didn't think Cupid would even leave me, right? He threw a few punches for me. That must have meant something.

I let myself drift into clouds with the naïve hope of Thor being wrong.

13

Spicy Conversation

Tuesday, January 26

Rainbows, and sunshine, and buttercream frosting, and congestion…lots of congestion.

I awoke from my fluffy dream wheezing and coughing, disgusted at the chest cough coated with mucus. Stumbling my way into the bathroom, I spat out whatever blocked my throat and coated my tongue. When I stepped out, I almost screamed.

"How did you get in?" I asked, placing a hand over my chest and leaning against the wall. "That's creepy, Thor."

"Are you sick?" he asked, his eyebrows furrowing with worry. "I got in with your spare key. I needed it to lock up yesterday." He flashed me the silver key before placing it on my dresser. "Come, let's get you back to bed and I can order you some soup."

"I already have soup," I mumbled, avoiding his concerned gaze. He touched my elbow and guided me back to bed.

"I know, but there's this new place that opened up and they have nice, spicy soup. I know you'll love it," he promised, ruffling my pillow for me and placing it back against the headrest.

Leaning back into it, I played with my fingers, staring intensely at the peeling skin around my nails that I shouldn't dare touch. But I touched it and I peeled them and withered in silent pain while Thor typed away on his phone, ordering my soup.

As ashamed as I am to admit it, Thor was the last person on my mind after sleeping with my date. In fact, he didn't cross my mind at all. Now that he sat in front of me, nothing but guilt suffocated me. This man had been nothing but good to me, and I went out and slept with someone else.

"So, how did this happen? You were fine when I last saw you," Thor asked, putting his phone down on the blanket.

I continued to fiddle with my fingers, and my heart rate increased. "I was out in the rain."

"That late?" he asked, the concern multiplying. When I didn't say anything, he put a finger under my chin and tilted my head up to look at him. The concerned gaze, so soft and caring, paired with the downturned lips was my undoing.

"I'm sorry. I'm so, so sorry. I slept with someone, and I didn't mean to. Well, I did mean to, but I was upset at you and Cupid. I mean, I have no right to be mad at you. I know you were telling me what I needed to hear, but at the moment, I was upset and the opportunity to sleep with someone presented itself and I took it because I felt lonely and I thought it'd make me feel better but it didn't." The word vomit didn't stop. His concerned gaze turned sad, and his blinking became slow with betrayal. His lips parted, but no words escaped. "Thor, please, you have to understand. I'm so sorry. I didn't mean to hurt you."

I couldn't think straight. All I knew was the damage was done.

"It's okay," he said softly, cutting me off when I didn't slow down. "Sophia, it's okay."

The apologies died on my lips, and tears from guilt glinted in my eyes.

"We're not even dating. You're allowed to do whatever you want," he assured me with puppy eyes that only twisted the knife. But he had a point. Why was the guilt consuming me whole when we weren't even dating? "I mean, I was kind of hoping to have a future with you—"

I gasped and my back straightened like a rod. "How can I make it up to you? Thor, you have to understand, I'm so sorry."

"No, Sophia, it's okay," he assured me, but his voice continued to hold the low pitch of betrayal.

"Please," I pleaded. I couldn't lose him. He was my only chance at falling in love, Cupid keeping his job, and thirty other people not being loveless for the rest of their lives. He wasn't that bad. He'd proven that he truly has changed. He'd been looking out for me when I couldn't look out for myself, and he'd been taking care of me, something he failed to do when we were dating.

"Well, there is one thing, but it may be asking for a lot," he said sheepishly. "You don't have to do it."

"No, I'll do anything," I promised. How could I hurt him like that? Where had my shame disappeared to?

"I want this relationship to work," he said, his hand caressing my leg, but it was a lot rougher than normal. I tried not to wince. "I know we aren't dating, but we can take it slow. I'll do anything for you, Sophia. I just need you back, but with you recently sleeping with random people and continuing to see Cupid, I'm a little conflicted."

He hinted at his past, in which his girlfriend before me cheated on him.

My eyebrows furrowed. "But I'm loyal. You know that. I was with you for a year."

"Yes, you were," he agreed, his eyes continuing to hold mine, "but people change."

My god, he was my only chance at love. "I'll stop seeing Cupid." The words trembled out before I could stop them, and I regretted them before they fully left my mouth

"I don't want you to do that," he said quickly, sitting up straight. "But if that's what you want to do, it would make me happy."

I mutely nodded my head.

His chest deflated with relief, and he gave me a small smile. "You haven't changed that much. You're still the strong-headed Sophia I know." The compliment gave me a tickle of pride that I stored away. "And besides, I think this may be better for your mental health. He's using you and has brought you nothing but misery. I can't imagine the pain you must have gone through after the sin you committed."

The knife did a 360, unplugged itself from my heart, and found a new spot to bury itself into. The sin I committed weighed heavier than an elephant.

Thor understood me. I didn't have to tell him how lonely and lost I felt. He knew. Cupid had yet to set me up for a serious date, which meant my time for finding someone was limited. I kept Thor around for safekeeping, but he'd shown he truly was a changed man and someone I would like to spend my future with.

When the doorbell rang, Thor excused himself to get the soup and I took that moment to reflect on how confused these past few days had left me.

Was Cupid the bad guy, or was Thor?

I sighed and leaned my head deeper into my pillow.

Maybe I was the bad guy.

14

Santa's Little Elf

By the time Friday rolled around, my immune system got back on track. After going to the doctor, getting prescribed medicine, and resting for the next few days, I was finally able to go on with my day without a runny nose or an ugly cough, which worked in Cupid's favor.

He came by Thursday evening and slid a paper into my mailbox, informing me of my next date. Several emotions burned through my body when I found the note pressed between two expensive bills.

The first was irritation. Irritated that he hadn't bothered to give it to me himself. Still, I reasoned that I had no right to such emotions, especially after the punches he threw for me.

The second emotion was a tingle of sadness I tried to bury because even I knew how unreasonable I was being. I couldn't help but be sad at his expectations for me to go on another date after the disaster of the last one, but I understood his position being on a time crunch.

That didn't mean I didn't let my emotions control my actions, though. If I had to go on this date, I sure as hell was going to make the most of it, and my first impression was going to be memorable.

After putting on my prettiest sundress and braiding my hair, I got to work on my makeup, highly inspired by clowns.

I dotted my nose red, along with circles of red lipsticks on the apples of my cheeks. I drew far beyond the outline of my lips and triangles above and below my eyes. I finished with my eyelids covered in red, sparkling eye makeup. It came out trashy but a clown nonetheless.

After locking all the doors, I jumped into my Uber. I came to accept that not knowing where I was going added more of a thrill and a hint of adventure to these dates. We rode there in silence, and I thought of all the places Cupid would have set me up.

Maybe this time I'd be riding high at the amusement park. Maybe I'd be swinging back and forth at my local park. Maybe I'd be cutting into a fancy steak at high-end dinner place or maybe I'd be lifting weights at the gym. The last place I expected was the hospital.

With a tired sigh, I made my way inside and asked the reception for Tomas Munoz's room. When I finally got to the floor and stood outside his room, my hands were filled. In my right hand, I held a 'Get Well Soon' balloon and balanced on my left palm was a dozen doughnuts.

"Tomas?" I called, stepping inside.

"Yes?" a muffled voice answered moments before the sheets pulled away and a brown face with wide eyes greeted me. His hand wandered around the table next to him for a moment before grabbing his circular glasses and slipped them on. "Oh, Sophia."

"Sophia? Nah, these days I've been calling myself Pennywise," I said, referring to the well-known clown people had not stopped raving about. I held out the box of doughnuts to him, which he happily took, and put the balloons with the rest of the cards and gifts. "So, what happened to you?" I asked as I pulled the uncomfortable plastic chair closer to the bed and sat down. "Cancer? Car accident? Mental health?"

"That's a broad range of things to pick from," he mused, pausing his munching on the honey doughnut. "I was actually in the right place at the wrong time."

"Yeah?"

"Yep."

When he didn't elaborate, I asked the teenage boy, "Were you at a girl's house and her boyfriend randomly came by?"

"Nope."

"Were you at the gas station shower when a biker gang came by?"

"Nah."

"You were at a club and the police found you, but you put up a fight and got hurt."

He snorted and pushed his glasses up higher. "As if."

"Your mom caught you doing something you weren't supposed to and got the whooping of your life."

He thought about it. "It's happened, but she's too gentle."

"Mm, I hear you. So, tell me, what happened?" I asked, leaning forward in interest. "You seem too smart to do anything dumb, so what happened?"

"I broke a rib by sneezing."

"What does that have anything to do with right place, wrong time?"

"I was in my room, which is the right place, and sneezed at the wrong time," he explained poorly.

I scratched my ear, processing what he said while trying to prevent a headache. "Alright, whatever," I said at last, admitting defeat.

"What's up with the makeup?"

"I thought I'd scare away my date but turns out my date is an idiot who broke a rib by sneezing," I said, shaking my head with mock disappointment. I gave him a tender smile, so he knew I was joking.

He huffed out a soft laugh before his eyes slid past me. When his smile widened, I curiously turned around. When I spotted Santa Clause, my smile slipped.

"Santa Clause? Is that who you're playing now?" Tomas asked, excitedly eyeing the large sack Cupid held in front of him.

"Sure am," Cupid said, coming to stand beside me with an unnecessarily large gap.

"Christmas isn't for another eleven months," I said flatly, keeping my gaze steady ahead and out the window.

"And Halloween isn't for another nine months," he responded, equally as flat. Neither one of us chanced a glance at each other.

The tension was so thick, even Tomas picked up on it. He eyed us warily, pulling the blanket up to his chin. "Did you guys break up or something?"

I laughed and placed a hand on Cupid's bicep, putting more force into the squeeze than needed. "Oh no. We're just friends. We had a minor disagreement. We're fine."

Cupid didn't say anything. He just brushed my hand off, setting a sharp stab through my stitched up and bruised heart.

"I'm sure," Tomas said softly, not looking convinced as he now eyed Cupid. Just as he was about to say something, Cupid cut in.

"Alright, so I got your gift—"

"I only want for both of you to make up," Tomas said, his lips turning up in a sly smile as his eyes switched between Cupid and me. "I'm a sick kid, after all. You won't deny me that, huh?"

After a heartbeat, Cupid wrapped an arm around my shoulder and pulled me to his side. He looked down at me. "Friends?"

"Acquaintances," I offered. I didn't want to be his friend. I didn't want to be his anything. He made that very clear when he kept his life from me.

Cupid's slightly turned-up lips for Tomas's sake dimmed into a straight line. "Acquaintances," he agreed at last, letting his bulky arm fall away. We both turned to Tomas, who seemed satisfied enough.

"Okay, now I want my real gift," he said, pushing himself up into a sitting position.

Cupid pulled open his red sack with one hand while adjusting his fake, white beard with the other. I couldn't help the smile, no matter how annoyed I felt. He looked ridiculous. We both did.

He pulled out a wrapped-up box and held it out to me. I grabbed it, surprised at how heavy it weighed.

"What do you think this is?" I asked Tomas, passing it over to him. Cupid put something else in my line of view. I grabbed the plastic bag, taking a peep inside and then groaned.

"It's an X-box," he said. Sure enough, after he had torn through the wrapping, he held up an X-box. While he excitedly gave his gratitude to Santa, I headed to the bathroom to change into the elf outfit Santa brought me.

Standing in the bathroom alone now, my calm mind started frantically pushing forth my promise to Thor. I promised I wouldn't see Cupid, but to be fair, I hadn't sought Cupid out. He sought me out. That meant I was still in the clear, right? Thor had no grounds to be upset, right?

My stomach twisted uncomfortably at the thought of sneaking around behind his back because there was no way I was telling Thor. For now, I reasoned this was all part of the job and Thor would understand.

Once the outfit was in place, I laughed at how ridiculous I looked with my pointed shoes, big ears, floppy hat, and clown makeup. I'd have to walk around with Santa, one month after Christmas passed. Was this what Cupid did for fun? Because I'd love to join him again.

A frown quickly replaced the smile as I thought about future meetups with Cupid. As if. Once he finished his job with me, I was sure he'd be more than happy to move on with his life.

The second I stepped out of the bathroom, laughter from Santa and Tomas greeted me at my expense, but I couldn't say I minded. My heart fluttered at seeing that genuine, gap-toothed grin I caused.

"Couldn't I be Mrs. Claus?" I asked while doing a little spin for them.

Then Santa said something that made my head spin. "Next year."

We stepped out into the hallways after promising Tomas that we'd be back, and I was pleasantly surprised to find a sledge waiting in the hallway.

"Nice," I said, giving Santa a wicked smile before jumping onto it. "Giddy up, Reindeer," I demanded, grabbing hold of the ropes.

"Alright, Little Elf," Santa obliged. He handed me his red bag, then grabbed hold of the rope and pulled me forward.

I giggled, holding on tighter after the initial jerk that nearly threw me off. We came to a stop three seconds later in the next room. Handing him his bag, we both entered and were greeted by a girl sitting on her bed, going through her phone with earbuds in. Upon seeing us enter, her whole face lit up like it truly was Christmas morning, and she yelled, "Santa!"

It appeared many were familiar with Santa around these halls because every child perked up and showed immense happiness. Even those who tried to keep up the façade of being too cool for

Santa cracked once he pulled out their gift. And it seemed he got it right every single time.

As we moved forward, one room after the other, I found myself looking at Santa for more prolonged times than the last with my heart nearly beating out of my chest. It was a good thing I wasn't hooked up to the heart monitors.

When we entered one of the teenage females' rooms, Kim, I found that she was busy skyping her friend and talking about the recent hockey game. When she received her gift, she thanked us pleasantly with a sparkling smile, and we took our leave.

Right outside the door, we found a guy walking past and trying to catch a peek inside Kim's room. Cupid stopped him before he could continue his walk.

"Here's your gift, Lu," Cupid said, his eyes dancing with a little humor.

Lu shifted his attention, flushing pink at being caught snooping. "Thanks, man. You didn't have to, though."

"Open it."

Lui opened it and the second he unwrapped the basket and saw the insides decorated with all sorts of hockey gear from the famous Maple Leafs team, his whole body started to glow with gratitude and happiness that I'd never seen anyone have before. After scrambling to say his gratitude, he did a pathetic job at covering it up and dashed past us and into Kim's room. When I heard her squeal, I realized this was yet another Cupid job.

At last, when we finished up in the last room, we walked around the floor gifting the staff, who seemed more than familiar with

Cupid and his acts of kindness. They sparked conversations that told me he'd been coming here for years. They were equally as friendly to me. It made me want to come back here every day, just to spread the cheer that Cupid seemed to do so well.

When there were no more gifts left and our task was completed, we slumped on the bench outside Tomas's room. Cupid pulled down his Santa beard while I took off my hat. The excitement and bliss slipped off out face and ran down our bodies until it became a puddle of tangled emotions at our feet with a cloud of tension hanging over our heads.

Could I make the situation any worse? Let's find out. "Did you beat up that guy last week?"

"What guy?" he asked, playing dumb.

"The one that made me run into your arms and weep like a baby," I said, leaning back against the bench and staring ahead. I couldn't meet his eyes.

He didn't answer for a moment. I didn't think he'd answer at all, but finally, he did. "Yeah. He said some vile things that made me knock his teeth loose."

My heart rate accelerated once more, and I found it hard to swallow. "Please don't throw a punch for me again," I said in a small voice. "I don't want you to get in trouble."

"You didn't," he assured me in an equally quiet voice. I turned my head and found him already staring down at me with gentle eyes. "He should have known better than to say the things he did. And besides, he wasn't supposed to take you home. Only chat you up and a little make-out session. He deserved it."

"Did you face any consequences?" He opened his mouth, and I shook my head. "Don't lie to me."

He sighed. "I just got a reduction of points but nothing serious. Don't worry."

With the tip of my toes, I drew hearts on the floor, thinking wisely about my next question. I could let it go and allow the tension to simmer down until he was ready, or I could just rip the Band-Aid off and ask him what I desperately wanted to know. If the odds were in my favor, maybe I could even get insight into his life.

"Just ask," he whispered, knowing the thoughts running wild in my head.

"Why do you check pulses? I noticed it the first time I babysat Noel, too. He was laying on the grass and you checked his wrist first before you came to sit beside me. Not to mention, you're restless in the middle of the night until you know everyone is alive." I swallowed. "Did you lose someone in their sleep?"

"Two people, actually," he said with a small, sad smile, turning away from me and directing his gaze to the lonely, white wall. "My mom died of sudden cardiac arrest in her sleep. She slipped away so silently, my dad didn't even notice until the next morning, when she didn't wake up at her usual time."

My hand just barely skimmed his pants, wondering if should offer him a comforting hand. He accepted it by putting a hand on top of mine.

"My dad died four months later by myocardial infarction, which is a heart attack during sleep that doesn't waken the victim. After my mother's passing, he started to take poor care of himself, and I think he died of heartbreak." Cupid squeezed my hand, and I realized that despite him usually pushing me away, he needed comfort right now.

Unsure, I slid a little closer and that was all he needed to wrap an arm around me and pull me against him. He lowered his head and buried it in my hair. "They had fairy-tale love, Sophia," he whispered. "They were so deeply in love, and I've never been able to see something as pure as that, even after years of working as Cupid."

"I'm sorry," was the only thing I could say. His grip only tightened, and we sat like that for a while, bathing in each other's comfort and warmth until he pulled away.

"So now I'm scared about losing others in their sleep," he finished, his voice slightly hoarse.

"That is pretty terrifying," I agreed. "I'm usually just worried about waking my cat with loud farts at night."

His lips pulled back in a genuine smile. "That's pretty terrifying too," he agreed.

"Not as terrifying as the diarrhea you took in my bathroom," I said, getting to my feet with a giggle.

"I think it just strengthens our bond," he said, playfully poking my side.

"Yes, I truly do feel as if you've become a part of me after that," I said sarcastically. Just before we stepped back into Tomas's room, I asked, "Cupid, what type of love is this?"

His lips turned up on the corners, and he looked down at me. "This one doesn't hurt, does it?"

I tilted my head. "I hope you know I don't blame you for Eros love, Cupid. Many people enjoy that love."

He stiffly nodded his head, but something told me he didn't believe me. "This is Agape love. It's the love of the soul. You give to the community or family and friends and strangers and expect nothing in return. It's selfless and for humanity." He put his hand on my back, nudging me towards the room. "You have a lot of it."

My head pounded with a threat of a headache. Cupid was far from toxic. He was kind and loving and cared about the people around him. He wouldn't hurt me the way Thor had in the past, but Thor promised not to hurt me again. Thor has been nothing but sweet to me, and looking out for me as I put myself into oncoming traffic. Maybe I should start putting more attention into him so when the time came, the verdict would be clear, and I'd have eyes for no one but Thor.

We entered the room with Tomas already facing us, holding up two movies.

"Which one?" he asked, shaking two Disney movies.

"Both, duh," I answered, grabbing the closest one and walking to the television.

While I set it up, Tomas cracked a joke. "Wanna know why Santa's sack is so big?"

"Why?" Cupid and I asked in unison.

"Because he only comes once a year."

Cupid seemed to understand the joke instantly and while he guffawed, I struggled.

"*Comes* once a year," Tomas emphasized, staring at me like I didn't know what one plus one was.

"OH!" I gasped. "Tomas, I'm telling your mother!" But even I couldn't help my laughter.

We spent the rest of the day with Tomas, watching movies, pigging out on fast food and candy, and tossing insults and jokes back and forth among us all. It felt like Christmas with the light, fun energy crackling between us and the atmosphere was filled with love and fondness after contributing and giving back to society.

Maybe I could convince Cupid to volunteer at the local food drive with me. I'd been wanting to do it for ages but never got around to it. That would be fun.

15

Not a Date

Monday, February 1

Green apple or red apple?

Green apples have more fiber and fewer carbohydrates, but red apples are sweet and have antioxidants.

Putting both down, I decided I'd just get Sour Patch Kids.

"Red apples. Always red apples."

Turning, I frowned at Cupid, watching him grab a plastic bag and started to fill it with red apples.

"How do you always find me?" I asked in amazement. He tied the bag up and dropped it into my cart while I continued to stare.

"You have a pretty steady schedule," he answered, grabbing my cart and pushing it forward.

"Don't you have better things to do?" I asked suspiciously, stopping at the onions.

"No," he answered. "Well, yeah but also no. Kind of in between. I had to talk to you about your next date."

My stomach dropped, and my breathing slowed. "Next date?"

"Well, I have fourteen days left, and you still haven't fallen in love, have you?" he asked pointedly.

"No one falls in love in fourteen days," I answered.

"Yes, but they do catch feeling in less than fourteen days, and that's all I need."

"Don't you need to set me up with a lifelong partner?" I asked with uncertainty. Something about going on a real date now didn't sit right. "I don't think I'm emotionally available right now."

"Yeah, you are," he said, grabbing the bag and tying it for me. "You have to be."

"Or else you get fired," I said flatly.

"Don't do that. You know it's more than just that. I keep my job and you find a lifelong partner," he stated like it's as easy as A-B-C. "Now, all you have to do is pick any person you want to go on a date with and I'll make it happen.

You.

The unwelcomed thought came unprovoked and before he even completed his sentence. My eyes widened, and I turned away so he couldn't see my face. That was not an appropriate thought.

"Take your time," he said, continuing to follow me around.

I continued to chastise myself for such thoughts while finishing up the quick grocery trip. The answer was simple. I should tell Cupid I was seeing Thor and be finished with all of this. Cupid would leave me forever and continue with his life. But I couldn't bring myself to do it. I wanted to savor it for as long as possible, even if that was going directly against what Thor wanted, but he said we weren't official, so I was pleased to do as I wanted. It wasn't like I was dating Cupid. We're just friends, after all.

Messy, messy, messy.

After I checked out, Cupid rolled my cart to its respective place and helped grab my bags. "I have my car," he said when we stepped outside.

"Oh, it's okay. I'll just get an Uber. I wanted to eat by—"

"Right. The Sugar and Sweets Bakeshop," he remembered, still walking to his car. "I've always wanted to try it."

Were we going on a…date?

Of course not. He would never go on a date with me. Just because he opened up to me in the hospital after showing me what a great person he was by going out of his way to make children's day and making the staff blush and the elderly grin didn't mean he liked me like that. I just think we upgraded from acquaintances to friends in his head, and that's where he drew the line.

"How do you know my whole schedule? Have you been stalking me since I was sixteen?" I asked, curling my lips up in mock disgust. "You pervert."

He chuckled and flickered my ear. "Shut up, I don't stalk anyone. When someone is assigned to me, I get a folder with their daily activities, their likes and dislikes, preferences, and history."

"Who does all that?" I asked.

"Cupid—the real one—and the committee," he answered nonchalantly, as if he wasn't telling me about something mythical and abnormal.

"That's so unreal. I don't think I've even processed this whole thing." Why it took me so long to realize how fake this sounded confused me as much as it did the next person. "So, you're telling me Cupid really does exist and he isn't a myth? That there's unknown power you harvest, and there's this unknown committee for love that gathers information on billions of people and sends some your way?"

"Exactly," he said with a smirk. "Complicated, I know. That's a part of the unknown world many ignore. You believe in God, angels, devils, hell, and heaven but when it comes to Cupid, all is lost to you."

"Yeah, but that's like believing in Santa," I point out, starting to hike the groceries into the trunk with Cupid.

"And who said that fat man doesn't exist?" He had a point.

"Have you ever met the real Cupid?"

Cupid's smirk widened. "He loves me, Sophia. We only met once, but he's the reason I haven't officially been kicked off for foolish behavior. When you have his protection, it's hard to get hurt, but it doesn't mean it won't happen."

"Like you getting fired for not making me fall in love," I stated. "That's a hell of a responsibility on me."

"And me," he said, giving me a nudge. "Your love life is in my hands."

After putting everything away, we started walking a street over to the bakery while I listed off all the good sweets they had, along with my favorites.

"I'd stay away from their peppermint cake bites. They taste like weed edibles. I've never tried weed edibles, but I assume that's what it tastes like. Or maybe chewing on a medicine pill. Or maybe a Xanax tab. I don't know, but what I do know is that it tastes horrible," I explained as we neared. "I'd try their La Rocca Cheesecake." I reached for the handle to hold the door open for him, but he beat me to it. "Oh." I blushed and stepped through. "Thank you."

Not a date. Not a date.

"Okay, order for me," Cupid said when we got in line at the busy bakery with the welcoming wafting smell of sugar and sweets. "Surprise me."

"You trust me to surprise you?" I asked, glancing back at him and stifling a laugh.

His eyes widened, and he shook his head. "Never mind."

"No, wait! Let me order. I promise I won't pick anything bad," I pleaded, widening my eyes and lifting my shoulders.

He reluctantly agreed, and I grinned. When it was my turn, I stepped up.

"Hey! Can I get German cheese square, walnut square, a slice of hazelnut buttercream cake, and mini cherry cheesecake, please," I said. "Debit." I reached for my purse, looking for my card and just as I grasped it, she put out the debit machine and Cupid gracefully tapped his card. I gasped and tried to swipe his hand away, but the transaction already took place. "Cupid, that was supposed to be on me," I snapped angrily, turning to shoot him a dark glare.

"This one's on me," he said, his eyes twinkling with humor. He reached past me and grabbed our wrapped-up dessert before walking away.

This is not a date, I told myself. This is not a date.

I sullenly followed him, genuinely upset I didn't get to treat him.

"That wasn't fair," I said when we both sat down at a cute table for two.

"Yes, it was," he said simply, pulling open the box. "I'm excited to try these." He used the plastic butter knife to cut everything in half. Then he picked up the cheesecake and surprised me by holding it up to my lips. I reeled back in surprise. "You have to try it first for me to know you're not playing with me," he explained.

"Oh." I reached to grab it from his hand, but he shook his head and placed it right against my lips, nudging them open. "uhamgowd," I choked out when he stuffed the whole half into my mouth. "Cupid!"

He just fed me.

Not a date. NOT A DATE!

"Mmm, yum," I made a show of chomping with my mouth open and rubbing my belly with satisfaction. "It's soooo good," I moaned, then stuck my tongue out so he could see chewed up piece in my mouth.

"Classy," he said just as a chewed-up piece fell out of my mouth.

My face burned with embarrassment. I grabbed the nearest napkin and picked it up. "You wanna try it?" I asked, holding the soggy piece to his lips.

"Yes please," he said and opened his mouth.

I threw my head back and laughed while lowering my hand. It was getting harder and harder to convince myself this wasn't the greatest date I've been on.

"Okay, I need you to do something," Cupid said when I finally settled down. I raised an eyebrow. "It seems you suck at taking rejection, so in the next thirty minutes, you have to be rejected by ten people. It can be any form of rejection, whether it's romantic or not. Just get rejected."

I titled my head to the side, my eyebrows drawing inwards. "And why on Earth would I do that?"

"If you do it, I'll let you babysit Noel again," he bargained.

"Wow, I definitely can't say no to that one, huh?" I asked sarcastically.

"What do you want?" he asked, folding his hands and putting them on the table. "I'm willing to give anything as long as you do this."

"Wow," I mumbled. "Consider this even for buying my food."

"You're weird about money, aren't you?" Cupid asked, surprised by my words.

"What?"

"Alex told me how you were so startled when the girls bought you movies and medicine and also made your food. Are you not used to being taken care of or looked after?"

"I…The only people that ever looked after me was my family. And anytime I went on a date, I refused to let any of the men pay after an incident where one of them wanted something in exchange for paying for the date. I never wanted to put myself in that position again," I answered, putting myself in a vulnerable position now that I had opened up.

"I would never do that," he responded, almost offended. "You've known me long enough to know that, right?" His eyebrows drew in, his eyes searching mine.

It was like he didn't believe his words unless I permitted him to. We were both vulnerable right now, seeking each other's comfort.

"Of course, I do," I said at last. "Hell, I also know you'd throw a punch for me at the guy who expected something in return for paying for my food."

He eased up then, his shoulders relaxing and his lips turning up slightly. He pulled out his phone and started the timer. "You have thirty minutes."

"This is about to be humiliating," I said, flattening down my shirt.

"I have faith in you," he encouraged.

Faith from Cupid was all I needed right now.

16

One Out Of A Million

Monday, February 1

Breathe in, breathe out. In, out. Breathe.

With one last pleading look at Cupid's amused face, I huffed out a breath and exited the bakery. Once outside, I found a hidden corner and leaned back against it. While I tried to calm my racing heart, I waited for my unsuspecting victim. When a group of loud teens walked by, I melted against the brick, hoping they didn't see me. When a man in business attire briskly walked past, I decided not to bother him. When a woman with a baby stroller strolled past, I pounced.

"Hi," I said, catching up with the woman and tapping her shoulder.

She paused and looked back at me. "Hi," she said, giving me a kind smile.

"Um, I'm sorry to bother you but I was wondering if I could borrow a hundred dollars," I asked, nervously playing with the ends of my hair.

"A hundred dollars?" she asked, her eyebrows drawing in and a concerned look etching onto her face. "What for?"

"Oh, you know…" I trailed off, trying to come up with a lie. "I need to, uh, pump my bike." A hundred dollars to pump my bike. Good one, you smart shit head.

She just stared at me for a moment, her grip on the stroller tightening with worry.

"You can say no," I whispered, willing for her to just rip the Band-Aid off and stop staring at me like I had two heads. Or that I was going to kidnap her baby. I'm not sure which is worse. What I am sure about is the growing sweat stain under my pits and my smile turning stale.

"I don't carry that much on me, I'm sorry." Without waiting for a response, she turned and strode away.

Feeling the burn of humiliation on my face, I reentered the bakery and slumped down in front of Cupid, who smirked with satisfaction.

"That was so bad, Cupid," I mumbled, burying my head in my hands. "I wanted the floor to open up and swallow me. I would have preferred to be bitten by a venomous snake than do that again."

"It's too bad the ground doesn't just spontaneously open up, nor do we have a venomous snake with us, which means you have to go back and get rejected nine more times. Time's running out."

Swallowing my fear and pushing aside the image of her horrified, disgusted face replaying in my head, I got up and scoped out the place. I finally picked my victims and walked over to the table a few feet from us.

"Hey," I said, sitting down elegantly on the extra chair. "It's my birthday. Can you sing for me?" I asked, getting straight to the point. No need to stall. I looked between the two men, who had been having a casual conversation before I intervened.

One of them looked uncomfortable while the other one's face lit up. "Yeah, I can," he said and rose to his feet.

"What? No, you don't have to," I said hurriedly, jumping to my feet when he climbed on the chair. "You can just say no."

"Hey!" he yelled, calling for attention to the rest of the people in the bakery. "It's this wonderful woman's birthday." He glanced down at me. "How old did you say you turned?"

"Twenty-six," I mumbled, meeting Cupid's eyes from across the room. His red face with a bulging vein in his neck told me he's one second away from exploding with laughter. I glared at him.

"She turned twenty-six! Let's sing happy birthday," he yelled to the people with blank faces, wondering what could be more important than their sweets and coffee. I waited for them to turn their shark eyes on me and glower with resentment for disturbing them.

"You picked the wrong guy," his friend mumbled, also looking equally as embarrassed as he slid down his chair.

"Happy birthday to you! Happy birthday to you," he started singing and people slowly joined it, their blank looks replaced with smirks and smile and laughter at the clear discomfort. The anger never came. "Happy birthday dear—"

"Sophia," Cupid threw in when the rest of the bakery went silent.

"Happy birthday to you!"

I raised one hand, showing my palm and then bowed. "Thank you, thank you," I said gratefully, although I wanted to die on the inside. I turned to the man who sat down, a full-blown, satisfied smile sparkling on his face. "Thank you."

"No worries. Always here to help," he said.

"Sorry," I said to his embarrassed and traumatized friend. I turned and walked back to Cupid, who let his laughter loose. "I did all that and didn't get a rejection."

"You know what you did get through?" he asked. "A birthday song and free dessert." We both turned as one of the staff placed a slice of classic chocolate cake between us.

"For our regular," the staff, Jen, said with a kind smile. "Have a good birthday."

"Oh," I said, startled. "Thank you." When she walked away, I looked at Cupid with wide eyes. "She knows who I am."

"Well, if you come in every week at the same time, I think it's only appropriate that she knows you," he said. "You can eat your cake later. Get moving. You still need nine rejections."

Sucking in a deep breath, I stepped back outside and waited for my next victim. It happened to be a woman around my age, walking leisurely while tapping away on her phone.

"Can I offer you a dance?" I asked, falling into step with her.

She paused and glanced up at me. "Sorry?"

"I recently learned how to slow dance, and I thought it'd be fun to teach someone else. You know, pay it forward," I answered, trying to come up with a reasonable explanation.

"Really?" she asked, her eyes widening. She tucked away her phone and stood with her hands at her side. "Sure. My boyfriend wants to take me to this fancy place for dinner on Friday night and he's a great dancer, but I never really picked up on anything."

"Really?" I asked, my eyes equally as wide. "You want me to teach you?" She nodded enthusiastically. "Fair warning, I only ever danced once."

"Fair enough," she said, watching as I took out my phone and opened google play. I put on the song I danced to with Lubin and put it on full volume, avoiding looking at anyone but her. The music certainly captured attention but having two people randomly start slow dancing to it made them stop in their tracks.

"Okay, so…"

For the next five minutes, we both laughed and stepped on each other toe as we tried to get our footing right and teach each other the limited knowledge we had. When we finally finished with the dip, she thanked me.

"I'll definitely practice at home with your tips," she said, tucking her hair behind her ear. "Thank you!" She leaned in and surprised me further with a hug. "It was great meeting you."

"You too!" I called after her as she turned and walked off, giving me a wave over her shoulder.

I looked inside the bakery and found Cupid just watching me with that same, small smile. I raised my shoulder in a 'what can you do' way before turning back to the people littering the streets.

Before my mind could catch up with my actions, I had fallen into step with a man who looked like he did not want to be bothered.

"Wanna go on a date?" I asked.

"I'm busy," he said stiffly, picking up his pace and walking straight past me.

I excitedly turned to the window and held up two fingers. Two rejections.

This went on for more than half an hour. I got rejections and acceptance, all of which I cherished. As time progressed, the less embarrassed I became with the rejections and willed for it to happen so I could just wrap up my day and go home. Cupid said this wasn't over until I got all ten rejections.

Along the way, I met great, enthusiastic people who were willing to take me up on my crazy offers, such as exchanging secrets or asking them to hire me for work. All experiences were memorable ones and not in an embarrassing way either. Getting rejected hurt a lot less.

When I finally had nine rejections, I sat back in front of Cupid.

"Can I get a compliment?" I asked. "Please say no."

"I like your determination," Cupid said with an evil spark in his eyes that said he wasn't going to let me rest until I died. "And you have nice hair."

Just a friendly compliment. Just a friendly compliment and nothing more.

I racked my brain for something else when an intriguing question came to mind. Before I could weigh the pros and cons of asking it, I blurted, "Will you go on a date with me?"

The second the question left my mouth, all regret hit with full force, making time freeze. Cupid and I just stared at one another, and everything in the background melted into nothing. It was just us in the store, both of us holding our breaths.

Cupid failed to answer, making the crunching in my stomach worse.

I breathed out an awkward laugh to break the silence, and Cupid's smiled widened, held up by invisible strings.

"No."

That's it. One word, no explanations.

It reminded me that I can get rejected a million times and feel indifferent to it all, but some rejections will just pierce right through the heart and leave me feeling like I was choking and gasping for breath.

"Ten," I said lamely when no other words came to me. I grabbed my purse. "Ten rejections. Let's go home."

If it didn't make me look so petty, I would have grabbed my groceries from his car and called an Uber, but I didn't want him to think I took it to heart. I might as well have done just that because I'd never had a more painfully awkward ride in my life.

When he pulled up at my house, I had to clear the air. "You know I was just joking, right?" I asked as he helped me take the grocery inside. "I was just trying to get my last rejection."

"Yeah, I know," he said nonchalantly, and I watched as his shoulders relax. He unpacked everything while I started to put it away. "I was just quiet because I had a few things on my mind." Nothing but a blatant lie. "Anyways, I need to know who you want to go on a date with."

"Uh, just set me up with anyone," I said, giving him my back so he didn't see how much that little question hurt. "Just make sure he likes driving and doesn't have children." For the second time in less than thirty minutes, I regretted the words as soon as they escaped.

"Before you knew I was Noel's dad, you were all for dating his father. Why the change of heart now?" he asked, his voice dropping slightly and the tension we cleared returned with such force, I tripped over my own feet but caught myself.

I chewed my lips, shifting around the kitchen and trying to come up with a reasonable answer. My silence must have stretched for too long because Cupid got restless.

"Never set you up with a single father. Got it," he said in a tone more aggressive than I liked. I turned around to apologize, but he was already out of the kitchen and down the hall. "You'll get a note tomorrow."

He closed the door with a little too much force, startling Sirus. I stared wide-eyed down the hall, all sorts of thoughts tangling together in my brain. As unlikely thoughts made themselves comfortable front and center in my mind, I wondered if I was reading too deeply into his actions. I had to, right? There was no way Cupid wanted to date me, right? Right?

Don't kid yourself, I thought. If he did, he would have set you up with him already.

Pushing away the pure disappointing echoing in my chest, I shot Cupid a text.

Me: *Don't slam my door. It has feelings*

He responded in under a minute.

Cupid: *We all do.*

We all do.

He even added the period at the end.

Maybe I shouldn't over analyze, or maybe I was analyzing it perfectly. All I did know was that I wounded Cupid's feelings.

The headache found it most appropriate to announce its appearance now, so I just put on a podcast and allowed their words to occupy my mind, so I didn't have to think about reality for a little while more.

Reality sucks.

17

Two Timing

Wednesday, February 3

As promised by Cupid, he dropped off my date's information early the next morning before I headed to work. I took a quick peep at it before throwing it in the recycling bin. Then I breathed in the morning air and made my way to work.

After work, with nothing to do, I took myself to the closest hardware store and bought all the materials needed for painting a room. Now would be a great day to set up my art room, which I'd conjured up images for in my head when I was young but had forgotten all about it when I stopped creating art. At home, I spent time laying down the drop cloth and taping down the switches, plugs, and borders on the wall. I set up the paint tray and dragged the ladder out of the garage, huffing and puffing the whole way up. As for the painting, I was going to start tomorrow, at exactly six in the evening.

The following day, after work, I shifted around the kitchen making brownies and two Rocher dessert bowls, which was a bowl made of chocolate with nuts on the outer layer and the inside of the bowl had chocolate mousse filling, with bits of Rocher inside for texture. Cupid made it clear when we went to the bakery that he'd devour anything with chocolate in a matter of seconds. I knew I couldn't go wrong with this. I spent the next little while cutting up and setting aside everything I needed to make a burrito for later.

With all that out of the way, I retied my ponytail into a high messy bun, put on my painting clothes, which consisted of sweats and an oversized t-shirt stolen from my brother, before starting on one of the four walls. Within half an hour of belting my music on the speaker and painting, the doorbell rang. A small smile graced my lips, and I turned down the music, allowing the soft instrumentals and Carry Underwood's voice to follow me out the room and down the stairs. Approaching the front door, I soothed my hair out of my face, then pulled the door open. The sight of a handsome face greeted me.

"Why, hello there, Cupid," I said, leaning my hip against the doorframe and folding my arms. "What brings you here?"

Cupid scowled at me as he eyed me without a hint of amusement. "What are you doing looking like a bum?" he asked. "You're half an hour late for your date."

"No, I'm not," I said. "I was just on my date before you interrupted."

He quirked up an eyebrow and peered past my shoulder. "Who?" he asked when he didn't find what he was looking for.

"Come inside. I'll show you," I said, stepping back. Cupid glanced back at his running car. "Turn it off and lock it. It might take a minute."

"I brought Noel," Cupid said, glancing back at me. "How long is this going to take?"

"NOEL!" I called, cupping my hands around my mouth. "Come inside!"

Cupid sighed and turned away from me. Walking back to his car, I watched as he turned it off before opening the back door. An occupied Noel exited the car, not paying attention to anything or anyone, promoting him to fall straight on his knees with his tablet skidding away from him.

"How many times do I have to tell you to watch where you're going, Noel?" Cupid asked, helping him to his feet and grabbing his tablet.

Noel tried to reach for the tablet again, but Cupid held it out of reach, grabbed his tiny hand, and pulled him towards the house.

"Hey Noel," I sang, greeting the scowling boy who looked identical to his scowling father. I don't know how I missed it. They had identical glares, identical hair, identical eyes. They're replicas of one another.

"Why are we at Buttface's house?" Noel asked, snatching his hand away from his dad's and planting his feet on the ground. He crossed his arms and glared at me through lowered brows.

. "Be nice," Cupid said, pushing the door open and entering while I stayed watching Noel. "Leave him," Cupid said over his shoulder, walking towards the kitchen. The heart of the house. "He'll come in eventually when he's done throwing a tantrum."

"Hmm," I hummed, watching the little boy glare up at me ruthlessly. "I guess you can just stay outside while your dad and I go paint upstairs."

Just like that, his glare wavered, and he unfolded his arms. "I want to paint," he called after me when I turned and walked away.

"As long as you close the door behind you, you're pleased to do whatever you want in here," I told him, and sure enough, he entered the house and closed the door. I glanced back to see him messily kicking off his light-up shoes.

"What's this?" Cupid asked, holding my Rocher bowl he pulled from the fridge. He pulled out the second one, holding both in his hands. "This for you and your date?" When he looked at me, I wondered if I imaged the jealousy.

"Put that back," I said. "Come upstairs." I glanced at Noel, who had jumped onto the aisle chair and grabbed hold of his tablet. I grabbed it from his hand. "Both of you."

All three of us walked upstairs. When we stopped at the work-in-progress room, void of any humans, Cupid said, "You're not on a date."

"I am with myself," I explained, handing Noel back his tablet but his attention was stolen by the open can filled with paint. He dipped his finger in and swirled it around. I peered up at Cupid with wide, innocent eyes and parted lips. "Will you help me paint, please?"

Cupid's lips titled up, laughter lighting his eyes. "You're sly, Sophia. You set this up, huh?"

"I'm just a genius," I answered, picking up the extra paint roller and handing it to him. "What can I say?"

"Sly," Cupid said, rolling the paint roller down my shirt. "Really sly." He walked away to the extra paint tray while I left to retrieve painting stuff for Noel. Once Noel settled with his YouTube video and his art gear, along with Sirus, who warmed up to Noel quickly, I joined Cupid, who occupied the wall opposite from me.

Guilt knocked at the back of my head, reminding me of Thor, but I reasoned with myself that once more, Cupid sought me out and I had no clue he would come over.

Alright, fine, I did set it all up, but Thor didn't know that, and this was more of a friendly apology than anything else. Maybe…maybe I should just stop seeing Thor altogether. I shook the thoughts away, deciding to fix the problem tomorrow.

"So, who'd you set me up with this time?" I asked Cupid. "Was it the undead? Or maybe it was an Uber driver." I paused in thought. "Can't say the second one would be a bad idea."

"It was actually one of your co-workers," Cupid answered after a moment of blank silence.

I gasped and twisted my body on the ladder to glare at Cupid's flexing back as he rolled paint onto the wall. "CUPID!" I yelled, startling Noel. "That's so dumb!"

"But you stood him up, so it's okay," Cupid said quickly, still not turning to look at me.

"No, that's worse," I argued, feeling my face starting heat up. "At least if I went on the date, I could have let him down easy."

"Did you not read the name on the paper?" Cupid asked, scratching the back of his head.

"I only read the paper to see the date and time. I didn't bother glancing at the name," I snapped. "Now what? I'll have to see him tomorrow and then what?"

"Say you got food poisoning, or you knocked out early for a nap and forgot to set an alarm," Cupid said, finally turning around. "Here, I have his number. You can call and apologize."

"What was going through your head when you thought you should pair me with someone I work with?" I asked, getting down the ladder and pulling out my phone. Cupid read me the number and I punched it in. "Well?" I asked while it rang.

Cupid shifted his eyes away from me and returned to painting. "I wasn't thinking," he said curtly.

"Hello?" a familiar voice answered.

"Hey," I squeaked, then cleared my throat. "This is Sophia."

"Oh…"

"I'm sorry for standing you up. I took a nap because I had this massive, and I mean massive, as in huge, headache." Cupid turned around and gave me a bewildered look. "It was bad. So anyway, I decided to take a nap to, you know, sleep it off or whatever because I'm a believer of natural remedies. My mom hated pills and stuff like that for minor things, so I could almost hear her yelling at me when I grabbed the Advil, so I chose to, you know, sleep it off." Cupid looked at me like I grew a second head, which made it only harder to focus. "But I completely forgot to set an alarm and I slept straight through the date. I'm super sorry."

"You can just say you stood me up, I can take it," Abe said with a chuckle. "I wanted to go on the date because I wanted to talk to you about your latest project. It seems big and I was wondering if I could pitch in a few ideas I have. So, it's not that serious."

My shoulders slumped in relief. "In that case, I'd be more than happy to talk about it with you tomorrow!"

"Well, I look forward to tomorrow then."

We said our farewells, and the second I cut the phone, Cupid said, "I didn't know you were such a terrible liar."

"My mom hated when we lied so I hardly ever did it, which has made me the worst liar on this planet," I explained, pocketing my phone.

"I can tell," Cupid said, his lips starting to stretch into a wide smile.

"Don't laugh," I said, giving his shoulder a shove.

"At least your future husband won't have to worry about you lying," Cupid said and returned to painting. Since he had his back to me, I couldn't analyze his facial expression, but I desperately hoped he was jealous at the mention of another man marrying me rather than him.

Damn it, I needed to get these thoughts out of my head.

"Cupid?" I called when I settled back on the ladder and resumed painting.

"Yes, Sophia."

"From here on out, how about I find my own date?" I asked. "You can trust me to fall in love or find my partner or whatever, I promise, but I want to do it."

"Why?"

"Because I have someone in mind."

"Okay," he said shortly.

"But, how exactly is this supposed to work? Do I have to make them fall for me too or can it be one-sided?" I questioned.

"The whole purpose is that you find your lifelong partner," Cupid pointed out. "The feeling has to be mutual."

"What happens if the relationship doesn't work out two or three years from now? Do you still lose your job?"

"No, happens all the time," Cupid answered. "They think they found the one and then fall out of love a few years later or the person changes and it just isn't the same, you know? We don't get penalized for that. We just have to start over."

Slowly spreading the lavender-colored paint over the white wall, my mind went into overdrive trying to think up a way to ask the next question. At last, I settled on, "Have you had any past serious relationships?" It was lame and straightforward, but I couldn't think past the tightening of anticipation in my stomach.

He glanced back at Noel, who was far too indulged in his video and painting to care about anything happening beyond it. Then he glanced at me. "No," he said at last after his eyes were done searching my face. "I haven't found my compatible other half."

"Why?" I asked curiously, tilting my head to the side. "Have you never tried? Are you assigned to yourself?"

"Yes, I am assigned to myself, which makes it harder. No one has really clicked with me, and even fewer want to be with a man who has a child," he explained.

"Mmm." I pursed my lips and tilted my head to the side. "I beg to differ. That boy is definitely a chick magnet. Have you seen how many ladies he pulls at the library?"

"Sure, but no one wants the responsibility when it comes down to it," he retorted.

"Completely wrong," I answered. "Women are nurturers. I bet women your age would be more than ecstatic, you know? Maybe you're just not looking in the right places."

As soon as the words left my mouth, I started to cuss myself out.

Damn it, damn it, damn it.

Did I just encourage him to go out with other women?

"But maybe you're right," I covered up quickly. "You're Cupid, after all."

"I am," he agreed, moving from his wall to the last one that needed to be painted. I joined him. "And what exactly do you mean women my age? How old do you think I am?"

I hummed thoughtfully, letting my eyes roam over him. It was more of a look of appreciation than an evaluation. "I'd say early 60's? It's the wrinkles that are throwing me off. You know—" I gasped when he flicked paint on my face.

"I beg to differ," Cupid said, wiping his wet fingers against his pants.

"Did you just—" I leaned down, dipped my whole hand in paint and tried to plant it right on his face, but he dodged me.

"Nice try, slowpoke," he teased and grabbed his paintbrush. He flicked it, covering my whole shirt with splats of purple.

"Paint fight!" Noel yelled, jumping to his feet and grabbing two bottles of the paint I provided him with. That was Sirus's cue to leave, and she did gracefully, trotting away from the mess, not wanting her luxurious fur to get caught in the crossfire.

"NO!" I yelled when he aimed them both at me. He squeezed, covering me with black and yellow before I could get another word out. Both his and his father's laughter echoed through the room and filled the house with newfound life.

I ran towards Noel, wrapped an arm around his stomach and kneeled behind him. "No more!" I yelled, holding him protectively in front of me, refusing to let him wiggle free. "I have your boy held captive."

That didn't stop Cupid. He splashed Noel, and I knew I had him. "Daddy's the enemy!" I yelled to Noel, letting him go. "GET HIM!"

United, we charged at Cupid with our paint, and soon, all three of us were dancing and ducking around the room, finding shelter under the lonely ladder and messy curtain while fighting for victory. The laugher only left us more breathless with all the running, slowing us down and weighing us with a disadvantage. The heavy scent of paint no longer smelt disgusting as we drenched one another in pretty colors that gave us life.

At last, when Cupid and I were bent over, heaving and still laughing, Noel took it upon himself to grab the whole can of purple paint and—

"NOEL, NO!" Cupid and I cried, but it didn't stop him from spilling the whole thing onto the drop sheet.

He glanced at us before—

"NO!" Cupid and I cried once more just as he dropped down and laid himself flat onto the paint.

"Look!" he cried as he moved his arms and legs. "A paint angel!"

"Oh, Noel," Cupid said, rubbing a hand over his face but he tried hard to push down a smile. "You've made a mess."

"No," I argued, sitting down on the steps of the ladder. "He made a paint angel. Didn't you hear him?"

"Daddy's deaf," Noel said, shooting me a toothy and slightly toothless grin.

"Daddy sure is," I said and winked at Cupid, whose face slowly turned a light shade of pink. I stared for a moment and then it hit me. "Daddy as in father," I said quickly, my own face mimicking his blush. "As in daddy who provides. Not daddy as in…you know. Obviously, you know, you dirty mind."

"Of course, I know," he drawled, walking towards me slowly. When he was close enough, he dropped his voice to a whisper and said, "Daddy as in gives sperm." My whole face went up in flames, and he seemed to get a kick out of it. "To make a child," he finished.

I wasn't going to let him have the last word. "Technically, that's a biological father, but there are fathers out there who have adopted children, so it isn't always the sperm that makes a man a father."

"Technically, I'm still correct in these circumstances." He bent over and draped my body over his shoulder. When he stood to his full height, I found myself staring at his bubble butt. Nice.

"CUPID!" I cried and tried to kick him in the gut, but he pinned my legs. "Let me down!" I beat on his back, but it simply made him chuckle, which rewarded me with his vibrating shoulders. "Noel, help me!"

Noel peered up at me from his laying position and said, "What do I get?"

"Oh, you little bugger," I said in disbelief. Cupid stepped around his son before lowering me down, laying me close to Noel.

I propped myself onto my elbow as Cupid lay beside me. I lay back down and our heads touched but neither of us moved. Our legs angled away from each other, and Noel lay in the middle of us in a puddle of paint.

Now that the commotion subsided into silence, Sirus found her way back inside the room, tiptoeing her way through the mess with a meow of disapproval. She found her way to me and climbed onto my chest, making herself comfortable there.

"Sophia?" Cupid said softly.

"Cupid," I answered, equally as softly. The chorus of John Legend's song, 'All of Me', played softly in the background, and I found myself on the verge of blurting 'I don't want to date anyone if it isn't you.'

The thought shook me to my core and made me happy me all the same.

Cause all of me

Loves all of you

Love your curves and all your edges

All your perfect imperfection

"Sorry I got paint in your hair," he whispered.

I tilted my head to the side, no longer looking at the ceiling. He did the same and now we were staring at one another, barely inches away. "It's okay," I whispered.

"Daddy," Noel whined. "I'm sticky."

Cupid seemed to snap out of whatever daze he had put both of us in and hurriedly pushed himself onto his elbows. I sighed and angled my head back up to stare at the ceiling.

"That's what happens when you roll in paint," Cupid said. From the corner of my eye, I saw him dip his finger into the pool of paint and smear it across Noel's face, which earned him a giggle.

"You can use my shower to get cleaned up," I said, finally sitting up.

"Thank you," Cupid said gratefully. "Leave the mess. I can clean that."

Nodding my head, I directed them to the bathroom and offered to give Noel one of my t-shirts, which Noel whined at, but Cupid accepted. As for Cupid, I had a spare change of my brother's clothing in the guest room, lucky for him.

While he tried to detangle Noel's hair and shower him, I finished up the last wall in record time and disposed of the drop sheet. Lucky for me, I bought the plastic one, so I didn't have to worry about paint seeping through the cloth. I removed all the tape and put all the brushes, trays, and ladder to one side. Fooling around and throwing paint at one another cost me different splats, smears, and colors on all four walls, giving it not only an artistic touch but also the touch of love. The room wasn't complete, but something told me this would be my favorite part of the house. I opened the window farther to allow the paint to air out before heading into the hallway, where I found Cupid instructing Noel not to do anything dumb.

"Come on," I said to Noel, holding my hand out for him. "Let's let Daddy wash up while we make dinner."

"Sophia, that isn't necessary," Cupid said.

"You guys helped me paint the room. I think I owe you dinner with no laxative," I said, throwing him a wink as Noel slipped his warm, tiny hands into mine. My jaw hung open as I excited motioned to it with my head to Cupid, who got the hint.

Cupid's eyes lingered on our hands for a second before he looked at me. "Looks like you made another friend," he whispered as Noel tugged me forward.

"Come on," he whined. Cupid disappeared into the bathroom and we headed downstairs, where Noel played with his tablet at the dining table and I put together the burritos for the three of us while making light conversation that Noel led.

By the time Cupid finally joined us, I finished making the food and Noel helped set the table. As soon as he saw me grabbing the plates, he put his tablet down and asked to help, which melted my heart.

"You raised a good kid," I whispered to Cupid when I walked past him to get to the fridge.

"Thank you," he whispered back when I leaned over him and put the fruit punch down in front of Noel.

Noel made most of the conversation at dinner, talking about class and homework and friends and teachers and his favorite show and a girl named Sarah that he may or may not have a crush on. The stuttering and blush gave him away and Cupid and I couldn't help the light teasing.

At last, when it came time to clean up the table and dishes, Cupid insisted in a stern voice that he take care of it. So, I grabbed my hairbrush and hair product and asked Noel to sit on the floor with me, between my legs. "I'm going to comb your hair," I informed him.

"No," he said without pausing. "It hurts."

"It hurts when Daddy does it," I said pointedly, "but you never let me comb your hair. If you never comb your pretty hair, you're going to have to shave it off."

"I'd rather shave it," he said stubbornly, swinging his legs back and forth.

"I'll give you chocolate if you let me try to brush your hair. If it hurts, I'll stop," I promised. All the while we conversed, Cupid had a smug smirk on his face that told me I would never win, which only fueled me more.

Noel thought about it for a second before sliding off the chair. I grinned with victory, and Cupid's smirk slipped. He pursed his lips when he caught my eyes before returning to the dishes. I started at the top of his hair and made my way down, all the while admiring the silkiness of the curls. In the future, if Noel properly maintained his hair, I knew he'd have perfect curls like his father, but since he never let anyone comb it, it was just a matted mess.

He only winced twice but didn't argue. Cupid finished the dishes and grabbed the dessert from the fridge after I asked him to. With two plates, he joined us on the floor and gave Noel a brownie, then spooned the moose mixture inside the chocolate bowl and brought it to my lips. I happily took it, and we all ate in relative silence with Noel's show playing.

By the time dessert finished, Noel's hair was cleared of all knots and left in a partially damp and fizzy mess. I held out my detangler spray to Cupid and said, "Works like a miracle. Take it."

He looked surprised. "I can't," he said, pushing it back towards me.

"You can," I insisted. "I hardly get hair knots, trust me."

Cupid lifted his hand, and before I knew it, his fingers found their way to the nape of my neck and loosely ran his finger through my open hair. With the way his eyes widened for a split second, I figured his hands moved without his brain's permission.

"I trust you," he said at last when he retrieved his hand. I pushed the detangler into his hand, which he reluctantly took.

Noel ran off to play with his tablet again, leaving Cupid and me on the floor in silence.

"Can I ask you something personal?" I hesitantly asked.

He raised an eyebrow, telling me to continue.

"What's up with Noel's mom?" I cleared my throat. "I mean, it's none of my business or anything, but I'm just a little curious because he mentioned he didn't have one when I babysat him."

Cupid twirled the detangler around in his hands, his eyes boring into mine. I held his stare, showing I came in peace. "I don't know," he said, at last, putting the bottle down. "Hospital told me to come pick up my baby. DNA proved that he's my child, so I vowed to protect him and take care of him to the best of my ability. I never heard from the woman again."

"Did you…I don't know…" I looked away then, finding it hard to meet his eyes. "Love her?"

Cupid chuckled softly. "Would it make me a bad person if I said I didn't even know her name?"

That made me gasp, then laugh. "Cupid, you're horrible," I said, giving his shoulder a playful push.

We continued talking long after we finished eating. Noel grew tired and fell asleep, leaving us to talk in hushed tones and stifle laughs behind our hands like teenagers trying not to get caught after sneaking into each other's rooms.

I told Cupid the story about the time I vomited all over my third-grade teacher and midway through the story, just as I reached the climax, Cupid's eyes slid over my shoulders and raised, as if looking at someone.

Wondering what suddenly made his smile slip and his poster stiffen, I glanced back. My breath caught in my throat and ice frosted my insides.

"Thor," I whispered as Cupid rose to his feet and I scrambled to mine.

All my self-assurance from earlier grew wings and flew straight out of my body, leaving me a shell of fear and anxiety.

18

Little Fishy

Wednesday, February 3

Even the sharpest knife wouldn't be able to cut through the suffocating tension in the room. No one spoke a word for a moment.

"What…" Thor looked between Cupid and me. "What the fuck, Sophia?"

"It's not what it looks like!" I blurted, throwing my hands out in front of me and stepping to the side so I could look between both men.

"Then, what is it? Because from here, it looks like you're hanging out with the man you promised not see again," Thor said, his nose flaring and his face erupting into flames. I took another small step back, not wanting to be within arm's length of him. He was one unpredictable man when he got angry.

"Promised not to see?" Cupid repeated under his breath. I turned my wide eyes to him, waiting for his anger to show, but he simply shook his head and turned his attention to Thor. "You appear hostile and are making Sophia uncomfortable. We'll both engage in a mature conversation once you calm down."

Thor glared at Cupid. "Stay the fuck out of this."

Cupid raised an eyebrow, his face void of all emotion. I honestly almost pissed my pants seeing how detached he suddenly looked. He leaned back against the counter and said, "Okay."

When Thor returned his gaze to me, I wished Cupid chose not to leave me on my own, but I brought myself into this mess and now, I must bring myself out of it. "Cupid set me up on a date and when I failed to show, he came over to ask why. I invited him inside and we ended up painting one of my rooms and eating dinner." I couldn't bring myself to say 'this is my fault' because I worried that if he heard the full sentence, he would blow up.

"You should have kicked him out," he said through clenched teeth.

I mutely nodded.

"You're a slut, just like the rest." It took me a moment to realize by 'the rest,' he meant his ex.

Unable to form any words to describe how untrue and insulting that was, I simply stared in disbelief.

In a matter of seconds, he was in my face, pointing an accusing finger at me and screaming profanities, one after the other in a jumbled mess. Some words I didn't know, but I figured they couldn't be anything nice. He'd never physically laid a hand on me before, but I worried that he'd test something new in his fit of rage. Just as I tried to step back, Thor was suddenly yanked away from me, and he fell on the ground with a heavy thud. Cupid stood protectively in front of me.

"Don't ever get that close to her again," Cupid sneered, widening his stance and standing stiffly.

Thor jumped to his feet, and knowing nothing good can come from that, I jumped in front of Cupid and cried out, "Please don't fight!" Thor had the built of a wrestler and stood a few inches taller than Cupid. Cupid wouldn't last longer than a minute.

"Get him out of your house," Thor demanded, piercing me with his cold stare.

"I'm not going anywhere," Cupid said calmly, rounding me and standing beside me. "If you don't leave—"

"I'll call the police," I cut in, knowing Cupid would threaten him and Thor didn't like to be threatened with physical violence. "Leave, Thor."

He opened his mouth to argue or maybe spit some more profanities, but at that moment, a small voice said, "Daddy?"

All three of our heads snapped to the side, where we found Noel staring at all of us with tired eyes. He yawned and dragged himself over to Cupid's side, where he hid behind his legs and peered up at Thor.

I held my breath, waiting for Thor's reaction. At last, Thor's hard, grim mouth curved into a smirk, and his eyes found mine. He mouthed 'slut.' "I want to see how long this last. Just remember, no one will ever love you the way I did." With a bombing, humorless laugh, he turned around and took his exit. He slammed the door hard, making myself and the house quiver.

"What happened?" Noel asked innocently.

"Wait," Cupid said to me as he guided Noel out of the room. "It's nothing, Noel. There was just a disagreement between us." I leaned back against the counter, trying to process what just happened.

When Cupid reappeared, he opened with, "So the dinner and dessert were for you two, huh?"

"What?" I asked, bewildered. "No, Cupi—"

"I don't care," he cut in. I wasn't sure if that was the truth or not from the blank look on his face that made my hair raise. "What I do care about is why your ex just walked in here, claiming to be dating you again."

I forcefully swallowed, knowing my answer was not going to please Cupid. "We're not dating, but we did agree to test the water," I mumbled, looking at my feet in shame. "After you told me I would be loveless if I didn't find someone within the time span, I panicked and texted Thor back, saying I missed him…" I went on to describe every encounter in detail, maybe adding unnecessary information, like where he got the soup from and how spicy it was on a scale of 1 to 10, but of course, opinions on such matters are subjective and based on how you ate growing up, along with the tolerance you've built over the years, but back to Thor…

By the time I finished, Cupid's face had softened, and he looked more dejected than anything. "This is my fault," he mumbled, pinching the bridge of his nose. "If I just checked your file every time it was updated, I would have known about him." He shook his head, mumbling a few things under his breath. At last, he looked up.

"Sophia." He grabbed both of my hands and sandwiched them between his. I stared down at our hands, unable to meet his warm, concerned eyes. "Thor has not changed at all. I'd prefer losing my job over ever seeing you with him. He's still the guy who fueled your rage towards your sister, made you cut your friends off because he was insecure, and distanced you from your passion. He may say he's changed, but he's still the man who pulled a knife on you when you said you were breaking up with him."

"He didn't use the knife on me," I mumbled. Yes, he did pull a knife on me. We were in the kitchen, and the knife was on the counter. He grabbed it and angrily pointed it at me, but he never got close enough to actually use it on me and I liked to believe he wouldn't, but there's always that lingering thought that if his friends hadn't come by at that exact moment, maybe he would have.

"I need you to make the best decision for your mental health and for your future, okay?" Cupid asked softly. "When he said, 'no one will love you the way I did,' think of it as a positive because the type of love he showed you is not what you deserve. You deserve happiness, love, care, security."

"Thank you," I whispered.

"I'll always be here for you," he promised.

He didn't seem angry. He didn't even seem upset. I had no clue how he felt, but I did know we were still on good terms. He scooped up Noel and bid me farewell.

My body still tingled with anticipation and fear despite everything having been blown up and dealt with. My insides rolled with disgust, mainly towards myself for even believing for a second

Thor had changed. I almost put Noel in danger, and that's something I would never forgive myself for if it had happened.

My body was ready to shut down for the night, but my mind was still rolling with all sorts of possibilities on how it could have gone wrong, how I could have avoided it. Maybe if I had locked the door or maybe if I hadn't invited Cupid into my house or maybe if I had pushed off my plan for another day or maybe if I had told Thor I wanted nothing to do with him earlier or maybe…maybe…maybe…

After locking all the doors and turning off the light, I headed upstairs to call it a night, but as I was about to walk past the painted room, I paused.

On the wall outside the room, there was a drawing of two big fishes and one small fish, all floating around in the water. How I missed that earlier, I wasn't sure, but seeing it now, I felt warmth spread not only through my body but also through the house. A touch of a child rather than artificial decoration was exactly what this house needed.

My body refused to fully shut down that night in fear that Thor would reappear and take his revenge. I slept with my phone right beside me and my phone app open, ready to call the police at the slightest sound.

The only thing putting my mind at ease was that little fishy.

19

Foe to Family

Friday, February 5

When Cupid came to me, delivering yet another date and promising that it would be my last, I almost put my foot down, but turns out, I would be seeing my parents. I'm willing to make exceptions. The note also stated to dress fancy, so I went all out in a loose cocktail dress and did my makeup to the best of my ability. Temptation urged me to call Alex and ask her to do my makeup but decided against it because my parents wouldn't pay enough attention to it. Then I hopped in my Uber and waited to see where the wheels would take me this time.

It turns out the wheels were not favoring my wallet. My jaw unhinged and my wallet winced just looking at the place. God, Cupid must have wanted some sort of revenge sending me here.

The place reeked of money and snob. It's a super fancy restaurant where high-end businesspeople went for meetings or something equally as boring and posh. It's the type of restaurant my middle-class tongue couldn't pronounce the name or the items on the menu no matter how hard I tried.

My phone buzzed with a text, but I didn't bother glancing at it, knowing it would be Mom nagging me. Picking up my speed, I hurried inside and spotted my parents without much trouble. When her eyes met mine, she shot me a disapproving look.

"You're late," she said as I pulled her into a quick hug and planted a wet, sloppy kiss on her cheek, knowing how much she'd hate that.

"By three minutes," I said, leaning over and giving Dad a swift hug, too.

"You should have put your hair up in a nice up-do," Mom scolded, wrapping a strand of her loose, artificial curl around her finger.

"But then we would match," I pointed out. "You look sexy, by the way." I let my eyes roam over her tight velvet dress that hugged her toned body perfectly. This woman really worked for her body and at this moment, it showed. "For a grandma, of course," I added when her face softened.

The scowl reappeared, and she smacked my back with her clutch. I giggled and stepped forward to the handsome man dressed in a tailored tux.

"Hello," I greeted him. "Reservations for Sophia." I figured Cupid would have the courtesy of reserving a table for us.

"Right this way," he said with a kind smile and led us forward.

I tossed my hair over my shoulder and winked at my parents. "I'm fancy," I whispered.

Mom stifled a laugh and shook her head. When we were seated with our menus, I asked, "What are you guys getting?"

We spent the next few minutes looking over the menu before calling the waiter over. Mom ordered for her and Dad with such elegance and precision, it made me raise my eyebrows. When it came to my turn for ordering, I stuttered a little and pointed it out on the menu. When Dad ordered alcohol, I had to put my foot down. "No, scratch that," I said, looking at the waiter. "No alcohol for any of us, thank you."

She glanced between my father and me before nodding. This was far too extravagant of a place to watch my Dad get drunk. One after the other was exactly how he'd take them, and nothing would prepare me for that embarrassment.

"I can handle my alcohol," Dad said when she left.

I swallowed. "I know," I said meekly, "but I figured it'd be nice if you were sober for now."

Mom blatantly rolled her eyes. "He drank before we came," she said flatly. "Maybe you should try telling your father a thing or two about drinking."

When I glanced at Dad, his face was stone cold, daring me to say something about his alcohol problem. "He's a grown man. He knows what he's doing," I said instead, not wanting to defy him.

"You're only enabling him," Mom said, her gaze heavy with disappointment.

I stalled for a moment. Cupid clearly got us together to talk about the underlying issues I had with them, and this fancy dinner would be an absolute waste if I didn't. "Mom? Dad?"

Mom tilted her head to the side and Dad continued to stare with the vacant look he always had. I wondered if he was even here right now.

"Do you love me?"

Really? I asked myself. That's what you choose to start with?

The nerves were catching up to me, and with the way my stomach was rolling, I wasn't sure I'd be able to force down the expensive food we ordered.

"Of course," Mom said while Dad gave a short nod. "Why?"

"I just feel like…you know…" I trailed off.

"Talk, Sophia," Mom said, her lack of patience showing itself.

"I feel like you just see me as a disappointment incapable of doing anything," I forced out and immediately shifted my gaze so I wouldn't have to look at them.

There was a moment of silence.

"Kids always disappoint parents," Mom finally said. "There's no escaping that. But they also tend to make their parents proud, too. Sure, I'm upset you didn't become a doctor, but I'm glad you're steady on your feet."

"But you're also disappointed I'm not married, right?" I prompted. "Or that I don't have children or a promotion."

Mom's lips slowly turned upwards, and being the mother she is, she knew where this was going. "You think we're disappointed because you aren't Elena."

I shrugged. "She's got a perfect life going, and she's smarter than me and much prettier too. She's also got way more talent and was better at all the sports you ever put us in. She's a model child, and then you have me."

Mom let a laugh slip despite her best attempt at keeping it hidden. She nudged Dad and said, "I told you we were the root of her jealousy."

"What does that mean?" I asked with a frown.

"We both always knew you've been a little jealous of Elena but couldn't figure out why and twenty-six years later, you finally admit that it has to do with us not giving you the attention you want."

"The attention I need," I corrected. "When I told you I bought a house, you ignored me."

"You were trying to steal the spotlight. That's on you," Mom points out.

"Fair enough," I agreed, only because I had more up my sleeve. "How about that time both of you went to Elena's fifth, eighth, and twelfth grade graduations but you guys alternated when it came to my graduations?" I paused. "Which, by the way, Dad never came to when it was his turn."

I remembered sitting in my chair at graduation, scanning the crowd and wondering why I couldn't see Dad. When they called my name, I got my diploma and faced the crowd like every other child had, pretending that there was someone amongst the sea of faces taking a picture of me. There wasn't.

Mom gasped and turned her sharp eyes to Dad, who withered into his chair, a spark of newfound emotion in his eyes.

"I forgot," he said lamely.

"Because of all that damn alcohol," Mom mumbled.

"It doesn't matter. My point it, Elena and I are only three years apart. When she graduated eighth grade, I was graduating fifth grade and both of you still went to hers but alternated at mine." I remembered locking myself in my room and crying the day away.

"We're sorry," Mom said at last. "I don't know why we did that, and I wish we hadn't."

"The only people that even came to my university graduation were Elena, the twins, and Kai. You guys forgot I even graduated," I said, my voice dripping heavy with disappointment. "So yes, maybe I am jealous of both Kai and Elena because they got a lot more attention than the twins and I did."

Mom nodded her head with understanding. "You're right. I think it had a lot to do with having to repeat everything for the fourth time, but I wish we had done it anyway because it may be the same event but it's different children."

"And you," I pinned my gaze at Dad, who looked interested in this topic. "Couldn't you just lay off the alcohol while we grew up? You didn't start drinking until I was around 4 or something but couldn't you have waited until I was grown and had babies before you faded into nothing?"

Mom cleared her throat, and when I glanced at her, I found her eyes wide. I realized how harsh that came off, but I was far too heated to care.

"You say you love me, but I never felt it," I admitted. "I felt like Elena was your favorite and you forgot about me half the time. I just...I just wish..." I trailed off and cleared my throat as my nose twitched with the warning of oncoming tears. "Why?" was all I could muster.

Dad put his hand out on the table, palm up. "Give me your hand," he said when I just stared blankly. I did as told. His hand curled around mine, and then he squeezed once…twice…thrice.

My heartrate increased, and my throat moved as I forcefully swallowed. An old, forgotten memory pushed to the surface, bursting in without much warning and immediately signaled the held-back tears. I squeezed back three times as a few tears trailed down my cheeks.

"I love you," he whispered, his eyes shining bright under the florescent light. The look in his eyes pulled me back into childhood, the part that I ignored and buried. The good memories. "I always have, and I always will."

Mom glanced between us, confused.

"One day," I started, my voice quivering slightly, "when I was at the park with Dad, we were coming back home, and he grabbed my hand and squeezed three times. He said it means I love you and to never forget it."

"I know I haven't been the best father, and I wish I could turn back time," he said, retrieving his hand and sitting back. "I'm sorry."

"I'll forgive you if you promise me one thing," I bargained, wiping away the tears as the food started to come. I held off on talking until we had everything in front of us. "Lay off the alcohol. Go to AA and get help." I rolled my eyes upwards to prevent tears.

"I want you here and healthy for when I have children so you can play with them and love them the way I wish you loved me."

Dad's lips thinned, and Moms' eyebrows shot up.

"Please," I pleaded. "I'm only twenty-six with a future still ahead of me. Please, Daddy."

There was a pregnant pause where Mom and I held our breath. At last, he said, "I'll try."

"Try your best," I said, reaching for the dish closest to me. "Let's eat."

As we ate, we shifted away from the heavy conversation and spoke about what I'm up to nowadays, along with future plans, and how things were going with my fake boyfriend. It got a little awkward there. Mom and I shared stories, and Dad commented every now and again. He was never much of a talker anyway, but it didn't matter. What did matter was that for the first time in a long time, I felt like my parents were really listening to me and cared about me. It felt like a weight being lifted and a burden being free. I didn't feel like I had to compete anymore, and all it took was a little talking.

They loved me. They were proud of me.

That's all I needed.

When I asked for the cheque, dreading the bill, the waitress walked off, promising to be back. I reached for my purse, but Mom had already got her card out. I frowned. "I got it, it's on me," I said, pulling out my card too.

"No, it's on your dad and me," Mom said, her frown matching mine.

"Don't frown, you'll just add another wrinkle to your face," I teased, which only made her frown deepen. "But I got this. Don't argue with me, Mom."

She scoffed and we both watched the waitress walk back, both of us sitting tensely.

"I got it," I said just as Mom put out her card and said, "I'm her Mom. I got it."

"No, I'm treating them," I said, pushing Mom's hand back and holding out my card.

The waitress's smile turned into a grin. "It looks like neither will have to pay. The bill has already been paid off by a gentleman named Lyco King."

I tilted my head to the side and glanced past her. "Is he here?"

"No, the transaction took place over the phone," she answered. "Have a good night."

"That's your boyfriend, right?" Mom asked, giving me a wide smile that made me uncomfortable.

"Don't look at me like that," I said as we all got up. "I don't know what he's up to."

She teased me a little more until we were outside. I hugged and kissed them goodbye before getting into my awaiting Uber. The drive back home will take a while, so I decided to kill time by calling Elena.

"What's up?" Elena answered on the first ring.

"Uh…" Maybe this conversation shouldn't be delivered through the phone. "Can I come over?"

She paused for a moment. "Everything alright?"

"Peachy," I answered. To ease her nerves, I said, "Boy problems."

That didn't help one bit. "What's wrong?" she asked, fully alert now.

"No, nothing like that!" I quickly clarified. "Just innocent questions. Can I come over?"

"Yes, yes, please come."

"Alright, I'll see you in half an hour."

I asked the Uber driver if we could change directions, and she happily obliged. The more miles we covered, the higher my anxiety raised. This conversation was long overdue.

20

Quick Math

Friday, February 5

When the driver pulled up, I almost told her to change the address back to the original one but forced myself to get out. Walking up her driveway and up the steps felt like walking through quicksand. Eventually, I willed myself to knock, and it opened in a matter of seconds.

"Was waiting for you right by the door," Elena said with a small smile, opening it further and allowing me in. "How's everything?"

"Good. How about you and the family?"

"Lilly knocked out and hubby is also in bed," she answered. "It's been a long day."

I winced. "So sorry."

"No, no," she said quickly. "Long day for them. I still got a spring in my step."

I winced again but for another reason. "Please don't say that again. You sound like a loser."

She laughed, and we both took a seat in her elegantly designed living room. Ever the perfectionist, not a thing peeped out of place and Lilly's toys were all neatly put away. "So, what's up?"

"I wanted to say sorry," I began, "for being the worst sister ever. I always looked at you through lenses of competition, and it became so bad that it turned into jealousy. I don't know why you even dealt with my bitter attitude for this long, but you did, and I couldn't be more grateful."

Opening up and looking past the haze of overwhelming sadness and anger, I saw other memories, such as when she helped me move into my new house, or when she jumped onto her chair during my university graduation and cheered the loudest for me. No matter the events that took place in my life, she made herself front and center, regardless of how far I pushed her away or the nasty things I said. I remember crying in her arms after some jerk in elementary school pushed me off the swings.

Elena blinked slowly at me, her lips parting in awe. Then, she opened her arms. I didn't waste a second burying myself in her comforting arms that always whispered safety and serenity since the beginning of time.

"I'd be lying if I said I didn't do some things to get a raise out of you. You're just so easy to anger," she whispered into my hair, her body shaking with a soft giggle. "Remember that time I put weed in your coin jar and then told Mom?"

I frowned. "How could I forget? She didn't let me go to formal."

Elena squeezed me tighter. "I did it because I was mad Mom took you shopping for a dress but didn't bother doing that with me."

"Elena!"

"What? Don't act like you wanted to go anyways."

"But still…"

"I'm sorry," she said, pulling back and holding me at arm's length. "But are we really gonna stand here and act like you didn't end up putting that weed right back in my car and call the cops?"

I gave her a cheeky grin. "But they never found it, remember?"

Elena ended up putting that weed inside my high school locker and telling my principal. I got hold of it before he did and hid it. That weed and us had been through a lot together, and in the end, when we called a truce, we smoked it together in the backyard when our parents weren't home. Dangerous games but good memories.

We both shared a laugh, one that clouded between us like a breath of fresh air and promised a new beginning. It'd been a while since I had shared a genuine laugh with her, and I couldn't say I didn't like it.

She tucked a piece of my hair behind my ear and gazed at me with nothing but love in her eyes. "As for that boy…" she asked softly, dropping her hand. "Is it Lyco? Is he…"

"No," I said quickly. "No. Lyco would never do that to me."

I didn't blame Elena for drawing a negative conclusion. Ever since Thor, Elena always had her guard up when I talked about a guy to her, which I hardly did but sometimes, it slipped.

I remembered exactly how Elena swooped in when she noticed me starting to get distant while in a relationship with Thor. She was the first to notice me drift away, and when she tried to confront me, I told her she was jealous of my happy, steady relationship and just because her boyfriends cheated on her didn't mean we were all unhappy. Fast forward a few months and she's the one who held me as I cried myself raw and she's the one who popped all his wheels, vandalized the front of his house, and sat behind bars for a day for me.

Before I could weigh the pros and cons, I found myself spilling everything happening with Cupid. I explained his position and my position and our position. "…but I'm supposed to be falling in love with someone that will be compatible and with me for the rest of my life but, Elena, I think…I think I'm falling for him. I don't think I love him or anything, but I've never, in my entire life, felt like this for anyone. He makes me crazy thinking about him. Every night, I sleep with him front and center of my mind, and when I'm not with him, I'm always wondering when I'll see him next and did I mention he has a child? The best one, too. I love Noel. But anyway, my problem is that to him, this is business, but to me, I have feelings for him. How do I get him to reciprocate?"

"Wow," Elena said, leaning back and rubbing her forehead when I finished. "That's a lot." I gave her a moment to process everything. "Okay, first and most importantly, if you get into a relationship with him, are you sure you're ready for the responsibility of being a stepmom?"

"Ugh, don't put it like that," I said with a flinch. It felt like knives poking at me. "It makes me feel evil. How many times have you heard people complain about their shitty, evil stepmoms?"

"Yes, but you won't be one," Elena said, putting a comforting hand on my thigh.

"Of course, I won't," I agreed. "Noel will love me, at least, I hope. Well, to be fair, I'd leave the disciplining to Cupid since that is his son—"

"Ah, ah, ah," Elena cut in. "No, you're going to have to stop that thinking. If you want to get with Lyco, you have to think about it as in marriage and having a future with him. That's how you see it, right?"

I thought about it. Was that what I saw? Did I want to get married to Cupid, have babies with him, grow old, mess with our grandchildren, and then lay in our graves?

My chest ached at the thought of losing him.

"I guess," I said with uncertainty. "I don't know, Elena. You have to remember this is just a crush or an equivalent to that."

"Okay, so then the first thing is figuring out if you want to be with him for the long run. If the answer is no, then leave the boy alone. He doesn't need a woman walking into his life, wreaking havoc, imprinting herself in his son's life, and then walking out, alright?" she said sternly.

"Got it," I said with a swift nod.

"Once that's established and you figure that you do want to be there for the long run, you have to start thinking about Noel. He's not just Lyco's son, he's your son too. I can't say much about co-parenting because I don't really know how it would work, but I do encourage that it's the first thing you talk about when you get serious with Lyco, and seeing how you described him as a great father, I figure he'll bring it up first and lay the boundaries."

I nodded slowly. Then I hesitantly asked, "What if he wants me to have no part in Noel's life?"

"I doubt it, seeing as he's allowed you to babysit and then you all got together to paint like a family."

My heart fluttered, and I felt my lips start to pull into a grin. "A family," I mumbled. "That's nice. Then I won't have to live in that house all alone. I could set him in his own room and the house could have more life and personal touches with his toys scattered and his jacket on the floor and…and…"

"Careful. Don't get too ahead of yourself. We're not at the moving in stage yet," she said with a soft laugh.

"Right, right."

"I would advise looking for red flags. I know you say Lyco isn't like *him*, but they all come in different shapes and sizes and smiles. If he says that you can have a minimal part in Noel's life, I'd say that's a red flag. It means he doesn't see much of a future with you and is looking for fun. Make sure you know where you stand and how he prioritizes you, alright?" she asked.

"Okay."

"Everything will flow naturally after that. Everything always starts complicated, but it gets easier, I promise," she said, gazing at me with that warm, loving look once more.

"I believe you," I said, putting my hand on her knee. "But here's the problem. I only have ten days left. That's a week and three days, in case you couldn't do that math."

She winced, her face screwing up with uncertainty. "Oh, that's such a short time."

"It's all I got," I said. "Don't make me feel like it's impossible."

"It's not," she said. "From your description, it sounds like he's maybe into you. I can't be sure. You go back on your word too much."

"Because I don't even know," I said honestly. "If he liked me, wouldn't he have set me up with him? I think I've made it fairly obvious that I like him. I love cooking for him and I enjoy his company and I tease him and even flirt a little."

"You said you flirted with him on the second day, right?" I nodded. "He probably is misreading and thinks you're only flirty by nature, which you are."

"I'm friendly by nature," I corrected.

"He might be feeling like there are mixed signals. You have to start to come on a little stronger. You have to make it known that you like him."

"Okay, but what if I'm reading it wrong and he actually doesn't have any feelings for me? Then he loses his job and I break my own heart," I said, feeling panic starting to grow within my chest. "This is too risky. Maybe I should just settle with some nice guy."

"Don't do that to yourself or that nice guy," she said, giving me a disapproving look. "And we both know that's not going to happen. You're too picky. I advise you to keep your eyes on the goal and don't skip out on a single day. For the next ten days, you're joined at the hip. Don't get clingy or anything. Just be yourself and let it come naturally."

"Elena, I have ten days!" I cried as reality set in and panic spread through my chest like wildfire. "There's no time."

She grasped my shoulders and gave me a hard shake that left me dizzy for a moment. "Get a hold of yourself," she demanded. "Ten days is a lot of time. There are 24 hours in a day. That's 340 hours in 10 days."

I paused for a moment. "No, I think you did the math wr—"

"Doesn't matter," she said, cutting me off. "What does matter is that it's a lot of hours, give or take a few."

"Take by a lot," I mumbled. If I was good at math, I would have spewed the right answer right then and there, but I couldn't do it fast enough. After 10 times 10, I blanked. "Oh, 240 hours," I said, snapping my finger and interrupting her motivation speech. "I have 240 hours to make him return my feelings."

"Are you proud of yourself?" she asked.

"Yes."

As she went on with her speech, I nodded my head, but my mind was somewhere else. I got the encouragement I needed for Cupid, but there was still another man I needed help with. Should I tell her about the one person she hates with a burning passion?

"What's wrong?" Her eyebrows drew in and her shoulders stiffened, bracing herself for bad news that she knew was coming.

"Who said there was something wrong?" I stalled, trying to gather my thoughts as fast as I could so I didn't say all the wrong things and set her off.

"Spit it out," she demanded, her dark eyes seeming to darken further with anger.

"I started seeing Thor again recently…" I trailed off when her face pinched together, and her lips pulled up in a sneer. I was sure her hair would light up on fire any second now.

"What happened?" she breathed the words out carefully, trying to keep her voice even and calm, but it did nothing to conceal the pure rage.

"Please don't be angry," I pleaded. "When Cupid came by my house telling me that if I don't fall in love in twenty-nine days…" I rambled on and on and on, telling her everything like I told Cupid, but Elena's advice would mean more to me. The longer I spoke, the redder her face became. "…Elena, I feel like the worst human ever because I just strung him along and now I have eyes for Cupid, who maybe doesn't even feel the same."

Elena undid her hair and started to run her fingers through them, detangling the non-existent knots. She dug her fingers roughly into her skull before pulling down with such force that she yanked a few stands lose. Her eyes were shifting between my face and the wall behind me the way they did when she couldn't contain her anger.

At last, she breathed in deeply and said, "I'm going to kill that good for nothing, son of a—" She bit down on her lips. "Sophia, don't you see? He's still the same bastard he was four years ago. He's still manipulating you and getting into your head. You may have said you'll stop seeing Cupid, but Thor knew exactly what he was doing when he took you down that path of conversation." The longer she talked, the harder it was for her to maintain her anger, causing her words to clump together.

I swallowed, my eyes starting to well with tears that I wished never existed in the first place. I was sick and tired of my tear ducts taking control when they're not welcomed. "I'm so stupid."

Elena started to pace the floor and I hid behind my hands. I promised myself I would never let a man do that to me again and here I was, letting that same man do the same thing all over again. I might as well join the circus.

When Elena was done ripping her hair out, she kneeled down beside me and grasped either side of my face in a firm hold. "Look at me," she demanded. I did. "Block him on everything. Don't ever talk to that boy again. Sophia, get this through your head: he does not care about you. He loves knowing he can control you and that you have a soft spot for him."

I slipped off the couch and fell down beside her. Without a moment's hesitation, I threw my arms around her neck and allowed for her body to comfort mine as I sobbed endlessly over my stupidity for going back to Thor and my gratitude for having Elena to comfort me exactly as she did four years ago.

Eventually, I calmed down and Elena made me a cup of green tea. I silently sipped on it while we both watched an episode of *The Office*. When it finished and my heart hurt a little bit less than it did earlier, I got to my feet and stretched my young body that liked to act old. We listened to my bones crack for a moment.

"Honestly, thanks for the advice," I said, turning to her as she stood. "It really helped a lot and…it felt nice."

She wrapped her arms around me again for a hug, which I happily returned.

"By the way, it was Cupid who made me open my eyes to how stupid I was acting towards you. It's him you should be thanking for knocking sense into me." We both winced at my choice of words. "Not literally," I said softly.

"I hope not, or I'll knock him dead," she promised, and I knew she meant it with her whole heart and soul.

"Elena? Please don't do anything to Thor. It's not worth the consequences." When she didn't say anything, I resorted to begging.

"Alright," she said at last. "Fine."

"I love you so much," I mumbled, pulling away just enough to look into her eyes.

"I love you so much, too."

21

Second Family

Saturday, February 6

After putting my phone on speaker while it rang, I checked out my art room. The walls were nice and dry and ready for my paintings to be hung up. The room needed to be decorated with art and set up with supplies, but I left that shopping for another day.

"Hey," Cupid answered a few rings later.

"Hey, Cupid," I greeted, planting my hands on my hips and staring at the walls. "I need help and was wondering if you're not too busy, can you come by?"

"Yeah, I'll be there in fifteen minutes," he said without hesitation.

"Bring Noel," I added. "I miss him."

"We'll be there."

After my talk with Elena, I texted Thor asking him to never message me again and blocked his number. He deserved it, after all. I had to stay focused on the task at hand, which was making Cupid take some form of romantic interest in me. It eased my nerves knowing Cupid didn't appear upset with me, and his kind gestures proved it.

For the next twenty minutes, I returned to laying my previous paintings and artwork around the room, figuring where to put certain ones and how to make it come together beautifully.

When Cupid and Noel entered through the unlocked door and came upstairs, I greeted them.

"What's up, Noel?" I said, getting on my knees and opening my arms.

"Ew, no," he said, hiding behind his dad. "Girls have cooties."

I scoffed and got to my feet, settling my gaze on an amused Cupid. "Do I have cooties, Cupid?" I asked, stepping towards him.

"You sure do," he said, putting his arm out so I didn't get any closer. "And I'm not trying to catch any cooties."

"Oh, you'll both catch it," I said and ran towards them with outstretched arms. Noel squealed and tried to take off running, but I grabbed him around the waist and laid a big, sloppy kiss on his cheek. "Now what?" I asked as he wiggled free and hid his bright, happy face behind his dad's legs.

"I come in peace," Cupid said, throwing his arms up in surrender when I rose to my feet and started towards him.

"Alright, I'll spare you," I said, only because I got too nervous to make a move. "What's that?" I asked, nodded to the Walmart plastic bag in his hand.

"For you," he said, passing it over. I curiously opened the bag up and found all sorts of chocolate and candy inside.

"Noel, look," I cried, getting on my knees once more and dumping the goodies out. "We can rot our teeth now."

"Daddy said I'm not allowed," Noel said sullenly, also kneeling in front of the candy and chocolate, gazing at it wistfully.

I glanced up at Cupid. "But it's the weekend," I teased, remembering Noel said his dad never let him have sweets until the weekend.

Cupid's eyes held a spark of surprise before he gingerly nodded. "Well, alright, but you can't fight me on brushing your teeth tonight, Noel."

Noel's whole face lit up and he dove straight into it. While he occupied himself with that, I got up and looked up at Cupid.

"Thank you," I said, referring to the chocolate and candy. "But why?"

Cupid scratched the back of his head. "What can I say? I'm a bad man who wants you to have diabetes," he teased.

"Mission accomplished. I'm going to fall asleep with wrappers all over my bed." We held each other's gaze for a moment and neither of us spoke. Clearing my throat and turning away, I said, "I need help pinning everything to the wall and whatnot. I already laid out what will go on what wall and the cut-out newspaper are the size of the artwork in front of it, so it will be easy to tell which goes where. Got it?"

"Got it," he said.

"By the way, was my date with my parents yesterday any sort of love?" I asked curiously.

"Storge love, the love of a child. It's love that comes naturally and effortlessly to parents for their children. No matter what, they'll always forgive you, accept you, and sacrifice for you." When he spieled this time, his tone held something tender and towards the end of his sentence, his eyes slid away from me to look at Noel. His eyes settled back on me. "They love you more than they'll ever be able to express."

I pondered over what he said, not taking this advice as easily as I took the other ones. "You think so?"

"You don't?"

"I mean, it's not always the case, is it? There's parents out there who use and abuse their children and have not even an atom of love for them."

Cupid ran his fingers through his hair and glanced at Noel for a brief moment before looking back at me. "You're right. It can get complicated sometimes, like when parents abandon their children. It's not always black and white."

"Families themselves are never black and white," I mumbled, turning away while thinking about Wade's sizzling feud with Dad. If parents loved their children as much as Cupid claimed, then surely Dad would do everything in his favor to get his son on his side again.

Before I walked off, he said, "One more thing."

I paused and glanced back.

"Alex told me I have to take you to her place, willing or not. She usually has movie night get-togethers with family and friends and wants you there."

"She wants me to come?" I asked, my mouth hanging open in astonishment. Even when I did have friends, I was never explicitly invited to anything, which is why it was so easy to just hide at home.

"Yes, of course," Cupid said, his eyes running over my face like he was looking for something. "Why are you so surprised?"

"Oh, this is bad," I said and rubbed my head. "Okay, we have to finish this quickly and then I have to go to the store to grab a few things and make dessert—"

"You don't have to—"

"But I want to," I cut in. "Let's get started."

Time practically flew right past us as Cupid and I shared stories with one another. It took a little prompting to get him to open up but when he did, I couldn't be more satisfied. He was full of life and energy as he spoke about his childhood and his parents. He spoke about couples he brought together and shone with pride at the mention of doing such a rewarding job for a living.

"Once, there was a woman in her mid-forties who had been so busy building up her business and hustling through the primary time of her life that she never got around to really investing herself in a serious relationship. Funny enough, I found her most compatible with the homeless man who was camping out in her building garage. One of the best love stories I've ever written."

"How…what? You're going to have to tell me what you did," I said, looking at him with wide eyes.

"Easy. She'd see him every morning and toss him a dollar. Saw him as nothing but beneath her. I threw him a hundred and told him he better use it to get a nice cut and clothing. He did just that and I pulled a few strings at the barber shop he went to. He got a job as a janitor minutes after his haircut was done. When he went back to the garage to pack up his stuff, the woman came by and angrily told him that it all belonged to someone.

"Don't you know it, turns out the only reason he wasn't kicked out of that garage was because she was paying top dollar to let him occupy that space and paid off anyone who had a complaint. When she found out it was him, there was a little bit of awkward conversation, but they took it from there. They now have a ten-year-old daughter and he's upgraded from janitor to financial assistant after some time in school."

"And all it took was a hundred-dollar bill," I said in awe.

"Alright, well, a little bit more than just a hundred-dollar bill. I had to sew the seed into the woman's mind that he was deserving of occupying that space, which meant talking terrible shit about him to the front lobby any time she passed by. All I had to do was tap into her empathy and when I did, she took care of that."

"How did you know they were compatible?"

"I had both of their files. Everything matched up pretty well, and their personalities were compatible. The most important part was making sure they crossed paths. Dropped a flier in front of him talking about that building and how great it was but, on the downside, a lot of homeless people hung out there due to great shelter in the garage. Not true, but he bought it and changed his location. That one was a work in progress but the most rewarding."

"Damn it. Here I was hoping I'd be the one who gave you the best love story."

Saying I was fascinated was an understatement. Cupid hoarded so much below the surface that nine days was not enough to explore it all, but I pushed for more conversation. We spoke about our flaws and our aspirations and where we saw ourselves five years from now. Noel eventually joined in the conversation after he finished his homework Cupid forced him to bring along.

All the artwork pinned to the wall were done by yours truly, except for two. Noel helped Cupid and I pin his two artworks into the wall, completing the room.

I left them at my place while I did a quick grocery run and then all three of us were contributing to the kitchen, making cupcakes. We let Noel help with the mixing and the icing, no matter how messy he got.

"You know," I said to Cupid as I helped Noel onto the counter. He had dragged one of the dining chairs over and insisted that the counter was the best place to eat cupcakes. "You're hard to get through to. Why do you shelter yourself so much?"

"Who doesn't shelter themselves?" Cupid asked, leaning against the counter and facing me while I unwrapped the cupcake for Noel. I handed it to him, and he wasted no time smearing the icing all around his mouth.

"Me," I said while giving Cupid his cupcake.

He chuckled, his eyes dancing with laughter. "After your last relationship, you never allowed a man into your life and you pushed away everyone who wanted to come back into your life. You're worse than me when it comes to sheltering yourself."

"Alright, fine, you got me, but I have a reason. What's yours?" I asked curiously, tilting my head. I fingered bits of icing off the top and into my mouth.

Cupid momentarily just stared, something he did often when he carefully thought about his answers. He's smart with his words, whereas I had a habit of running my mouth faster than my brain, leading to a lot of embarrassment. Then, he subtly tipped his head to Noel. "That's why," he said when I got the hint. "Inviting someone into my life is inviting someone into both our lives, and I can't risk it."

I pulled a bit of the cupcake off and popped it in my mouth, tasting the sweetness melt into my mouth with pure perfection, not to toot my own horn or anything. "Would you make an exception for the right person?" I asked, dancing around the clear question.

Cupid seemed to catch on just as fast because his eyebrows drew in slightly. He paused again, his eyes switching between mine, and clear worry starting to crack through his poker face.

"Yes," he whispered, and I could have sworn his head started moving towards mine or maybe my head started moving towards his. It didn't matter because in seconds, the moment was gone when Noel spoke.

"I want another cupcake!"

I cleared my throat and looked away, while Cupid shifted his attention to Noel, who had managed to get icing on his ear and even a little in his hair, along with crumbs all over his pants and shirt.

"You're the cleanest eater I've come across," I said and watched as he beamed with pride.

"I know," he said, his voice filled with cockiness similar to his father.

We cleaned him up, along with the kitchen, before I headed upstairs to change into something simple and nice while the boys waited downstairs. When I arrived downstairs, I found that Cupid had already taken the cupcakes into the car and busied himself buckling Noel in. Making sure all the doors were locked, I headed out and got into the passenger seat as Cupid got into the driver's seat. The ride to Alex's place was filled with us singing all the wrong lyrics and a lot of screaming from Noel.

I learned that Alex lived in the same place as Cupid, as well as the same floor, just one door over. Cupid informed me that their grandfather lived just across the hall as well.

"I never got a chance to ask, but I thought Lubin was in a senior home," I asked while we waited in the elevator.

"No, that was just for you," Cupid answered. "I did want to set you up with someone at a senior home for a real experience, but I figured Grandpa was my best bet. He's a great man."

"He sure is," I agreed. We stepped into the hallway, and Noel lead us down the hall, stopping right outside his aunt's door. Cupid opened the door, and we all filed in, where the party had already started.

I found Lubin sitting at the aisle, nursing a drink, while Alex, Olah, and Cece were in the living room, staring at the television and debating what Netflix movie to watch. I slid the cupcakes onto the counter and greeted Lubin first.

"Hey," I said, leaning over the aisle and swaying slightly. "How are you?"

"Could be better," he answered, his cold eyes meeting mine with that unwavering and uncomfortable stare he seemed to have reserved specifically for me.

"Can always be better," I agreed, "but can always be worse."

His lips turned up slightly and his gaze softened. "Can always be worse," he agreed.

"You have to teach me how to dance, by the way," I said. "I'm trying to woo this man, and I figured I'd take him dancing but I can't do that if I can't dance."

"Can he dance?" Lubin asked, and although it was hard to see, I could tell I caught his interest.

I tilted my head slightly and snuck a glance at Cupid, who was engaged in a tickle fight with Noel. Lubin caught the millisecond glance and looked over his shoulder, at Cupid.

"Ah, I see," Lubin said, his lips quirking up in a barely-there smile.

"No, it's not what you think," I said quickly, returning my wide-eyed gaze to him. "I swear."

"Okay," he acknowledged but made it clear he didn't believe me with an enthusiastic nod. "But if you're wondering if Lyco can dance, he can."

"Then yeah, the guy I like can dance," I said lamely, admitting defeat. I confided in him. "Do I have a chance with Cupid?" I asked, leaning in closer and dropping my voice. "Or is it hopeless and I should just find a man willing to settle?"

"You should never be willing to just settle, and neither should the man you're seeing. You want the best of the best for yourself and for him," Lubin explained. "Don't be foolish."

"You didn't answer my question," I said pointedly. "Does that mean no?"

"I've never heard that boy talk about women," Lubin finally said, "but since the day he found out he'd get fired because of you, he's never shut up."

I tilted my head. "Bad or good?"

"Frustration. A lot of frustration," he answered. "You're his little nightmare, after all."

"Oh please," I scoffed. "I made this job all too easy for him. I went on dates whenever and wherever he said without arguing."

"Yes, but if there's one thing to remember, Cupid's job is on the line and he loves his job too dearly—"

"And he wouldn't risk it for a woman," I mumbled.

"Now, I'm not saying that," Lubin said, "but I am saying that there's a lot on the line here."

"So, should I just walk away?" I asked, desperate for answers. "Should I leave him alone and try somewhere else, like this bartender that's single and nice? I only have eight days left."

"I can't tell you what to do," Lubin said. "Although, between you and I, Lyco doesn't hate you in the least, even if he comes home confused and tired after dealing with you."

"He always comes back confused and tired?" I asked, bewildered. "I'm hardly difficult. How do I wear him out?"

"I'm not inside his head," Lubin said, taking a drink out of his glass. "You should just talk to him."

"I should," I mumbled, just as Alex slid up beside me.

"What are you guys talking about?" she asked, nearly bouncing on her feet as she switched gazes between us. I shot Lubin a warning look, making his lips turn up a little higher.

"I was just asking Lubin to teach me how to dance properly," I said, standing tall. "Thank you so much for inviting me. I really appreciate it."

Alex pulled me into a bone-crushing hug. I returned it just as tightly, feeling like she was squeezing every last drop of anxiety, fear, and worry away from me.

"I'm so glad you could make it. You didn't have to bring anything, though!" she said after she pulled away and saw the cupcakes. "But Lyco says it's really good, so I'm looking forward to eating it."

I grinned at the back of her head as she turned and dragged me to the living room. No matter how hard I tried, the smile didn't slip. Olah and Cece were playing rock, paper, scissors over a movie of their choice, and when Cece won with a sweet giggle, Olah wasted no time tackling her and they both went down.

"You cheated," Olah whined, getting off Cece at her insistence.

"Olah, that hurt," Cece said, giving Olah a soft push that didn't faze her.

I slumped down beside Noel, caging him between Cupid and me.

"I want to watch Inside Out!" Noel whined, sinking back into the backrest and cuddling close to Cupid, who raised an arm and casually draped it over the top of the backrest. His fingers played with my hair, and when I glanced at him, I found him indulged in Cece and Olah's argument. Was he doing it absentmindedly?

"No, we're watching Insidious," Olah said, turning her gaze to the outraged boy. "It's a scary movie, and you're going to piss your pants."

"I'm not scared," Noel said with a huff, crossing his arms.

Olah dropped to her hands and knees and slowly crawled towards him. She looked scary as her dark hair curtained her face, only showing a sliver of her skin and eyes. Noel coward back.

"It's a story about a little boy who gets eaten by a monster," she said slowly, stretching each word carefully and ending the sentence when she touched the sofa. She jumped up and screamed "ROWR!"

Noel let out a cry and even I flinched back.

"Daddy!" Noel cried, burying his face into Cupid's shirt, who had a small grin on his face.

"The only monster here is Olah," Cupid comforted, removing his hand playing with my hair to comfort his son. "I'll always protect you."

Olah got up with a loud laugh and ruffed Noel's hair. "I'm just messing." I also got up.

"Hey, Olah," I greeted.

"What's up, girl?" she asked, her face lighting up. "How's everything been?" she asked as she pulled me into a hug.

Cece joined our conversation, and all three of us stood for a moment, just talking and catching up about trifling things before Alex called us to help with the snacks. The movie we settled on was *Inside Out*, and before we even got halfway through, I found myself starting to lose the battle against sleep.

I allowed sleep to blanket me with the warmth and love that radiated through the room.

22

Bitter Cupcakes

Sunday, February 7

With a soft groan, I stretched out my body, hearing the satisfying cracks, but something hard prevented me from lengthening my legs. My eyes fluttered open, and I found myself staring at a wall that wasn't mine.

Pushing myself up onto my elbows, I glanced down at the foot of the bed and found Cupid laid out horizontally with his head positioned awkwardly, still in deep sleep. As my mind finally caught up with the situation, I realized I was back in Cupid's guest room, although it didn't explain why he was awkwardly sleeping at the foot of the bed.

Before I could wake him up, the guest room door creaked open and Noel peered inside. "Why is Daddy in here?" he asked, stepping further inside.

"I have no clue," I said, eyeing Noel in his adorable car pajamas. The pants dragged a little bit and he had to tug them up so he didn't trip as he walked towards me. I lifted the blanket and patted the spot beside me. He glanced at his dad for another moment before pulling himself up and crawling under the cover, right beside me. I spooned him, loving his tiny body against mine as I curled around him with the blanket pulled to our chins. "Let's sleep for another while."

Noel didn't have a problem falling asleep within minutes, but now that my brain had flickered to life, I couldn't find myself going back to sleep. So I lay awake, thinking of something that may never happen.

Could this one day be my family? Could this be my future? I desperately wanted it now that I got a taste of it.

After about half an hour, I carefully crawled out, trying not to disturb them, then made my way into the bathroom. I freshened up and changed out of my dress, into Cupid's t-shirt he hung behind the door, along with his sweatpants. Humming to myself, I put the news on for background noise before getting to work on breakfast.

"Good morning," I greeted when both boys stumbled out nearly an hour later, both of their hair a frizzy mess. My heart nearly leapt out of my chest at the adorable sight of father and son looking identical. "How was your sleep?"

Noel rubbed his eyes, and Cupid just stared for a moment, with no expression on his face. "Pretty good," he answered blankly.

Noel walked away to sit on the couch in front of the television. He grabbed the remote and started switching through the channels while Cupid slowly advanced towards me, the confusion as clear as day on his face.

"I want pancakes!" Noel yelled.

"Your wish is my command," I answered in a deep voice. Cupid stopped at the aisle, getting a good look at me.

"You didn't have to make breakfast. I actually planned on making it, but I guess I slept in," he said, a tingle of embarrassment presented on his ears. His eyes slowly trailed over me, leaving a trail of tingles in his wake. "Are you wearing my clothes?"

"Yeah, sorry. The dress was uncomfortable so I switched out of it and grabbed whatever was behind the bathroom door," I apologized, although I couldn't say I was truly sorry. The whole time I'd worn it, I'd basked in his pleasant scent that kept the small smile on my face, no matter how hard I tried to push it down.

"That's okay," he said, leaning forward onto his elbows. "You wear it better than I do."

"Don't make me blush," I said, turning away so he didn't see the blush on my face slowly creeping its way up my cheeks. "What were you doing sleeping in the guest room?"

When I glanced back, I found that we were alternating blushing. His face made tomato jealous. I threw my head back and laughed, surprised at how easy it is to get such an innocent reaction I've never been able to prompt out of anyone before.

He scratched the back of his head, avoiding my gaze. "I don't know what happened," he said. "I came to check your pulse and then…I figured my room was too far even though it was only a few steps away, so I ended up knocking out on your bed. I'm sorry about that."

I bit my bottom lip to stifle a burst of laughter at how pure and innocent he looked right now. God, he resembled Noel when he tried to act sweet and it made me melt like butter on a hot pan. "I didn't mind. It was actually a pleasant surprise when I woke up."

"Pleasant, huh?" Cupid asked, his eyes shifting from shame to something new I couldn't quite pin.

"Very pleasant," I agreed, pushing forth two plates. "Noel, come eat." Cupid stood and grabbed the plates of pancake and French toast, while I grabbed the chocolate chia pudding for Cupid. We all sat around the dining table, eating and talking about the movie last night, in which Cupid gave me a secretive look that I didn't understand. Maybe he was aware that I had fallen asleep so early on. I didn't think much of it.

When we were all done, Cupid excused himself to get Noel's clothing ready for his shower and told Noel to get in the tub. Noel just took another pancake and cut into it.

When he was halfway done the pancake and wrapped up his story about his plans on being the fastest car driver in the world, he surprised me with his next words. "I want a mom."

My heart stilled in my chest and my saliva refused to go down as I watched him swing his feet back and forth while cutting into his pancake. "What?" I choked out. Past the sound of running water in the bathroom, all else was silent.

"I want a mommy," he said, looking up at me.

"Well…" I trailed off, silently pleading for Cupid to come back. "You don't just want any mommy. You want someone who will love you forever and ever and take care of you and will love your daddy too."

"Like you?" he asked innocently. The words threw me in a loop and made me chock on my saliva.

"Uhh…"

"Noel!" Cupid called. "Let's go."

Noel squished pancake into his fist and scurried off to find his dad inside the bathroom, while I sat dumbfounded.

God, what had I done? If Cupid didn't see me as anything more than just the nightmare of a woman who might get him fired, then things were going to end like shattered glass. Suddenly, I didn't want to advance in a relationship with him. The odds of him rejecting me were high, forever ruining whatever casual fun we have now. Ruining that meant no longer being a part of Noel's life, which hurt a lot more than I wanted to admit.

My hands fisted around the t-shirt, right above my heart as physical pain shoot through me. "Urgh," I hissed, bending forward slightly. Why did I do this to myself? Why on Earth did I come into their life? Why couldn't I just keep distance between us and fall in love with some normal bloke on the street?

Knocking on the door pulled me away from my frightening thoughts. Rubbing my chest, I walked over to the door and peeped through the peephole, where I saw Alex patiently waiting. Masking my worry with a smile, I pulled open the door and greeted Alex.

"Hey!" she said happily, stepping inside. "Good sleep?"

"Yep," I answered. "You?"

"Slept like a baby," she answered. She held her hands out, presenting me my empty and washed cupcake tray. "The cupcakes were amazing. You have to give me the recipe."

"Of course!" I said. "You have to come over for dinner soon."

"My God, I wouldn't miss it for the world!" she said, her whole face lighting up like the Fourth of July. "Cupid raves about it so much."

"He does?" I asked as my aching heart started to speed up.

"He does," she said, nodding her head. "He even loved the pizza you spiked with laxative. Great job, by the way."

My grin stretched even wider, and we high-fived like little kids. "It was a little bit of payback," I explained.

"Which he most likely deserved. Trust me, I know. He's such a pain sometimes," she said, rolling her eyes, which then quickly took in my outfit. "Ou," she said suggestively, her eyes widening and lips curving up.

"Oh no," I said, shaking my head and feeling my body warm. "Definitely not what it looks like. I just changed out of my dress into something much more comfortable, and since Noel's clothing don't fit, I got the next best thing."

"Fair enough," she said, but her eyes were still bright with humor. "I just figured after last night…" she trailed off, giving me that suggestive look again. It reminded me of the secretive look Cupid gave me at breakfast.

"What?" I asked, startled and suddenly alert. "What happened? Did I do something stupid?"

"Besides the fact that you practically fell into his lap during your sleep with your face a little too close to his—"

I gasped. "But Noel!"

"By that point, he had moved away to sit with Pa," she answered, waving away my concern. "We were all too amused watching Lyco squirm."

I winced and placed my cool hands against my hot cheeks, trying to even out the temperature. "What happened?" I whispered, unsure if I really wanted to know.

"Well, he fixed your head so you weren't so close to his crotch and then continued to act like it didn't happen. After the movie ended, he scooted you into his arms and declared that you'd be sleeping at his place, rather than our girl sleepover. He was very adamant that you stay at his, reasoning that you were familiar with his place, but I can't say that's the full truth," she said with a cheeky smile, leaning back and crossing her arms. "So, what's up with you and my brother?"

"Nothing," I said a little too quickly. She raised an eyebrow. "I swear, it's nothing. Nothing happened, I swear."

Her smile only stretched, and she continued to stare without words.

"Alright fine," I huffed, giving in.

"LYCO!" Alex yelled as she grabbed my arm and threw open the door. "I'm stealing your girl!" She pulled me out of the condo and into hers, where I saw the other two girls on the living room floor, still wrapped up in blankets and on their phones. "She admitted it."

Both girls instantly sat up, their faces lighting up to match Alex's. Alex and I sat cross-legged in front of them.

"Spill," Cece demanded, and I was a little taken back. This was the most aggressive I'd ever seen her. She realized and gave me a small smile while the other two laughed. "Sorry, but we need to know what's going on. I love romance."

With a nervous smile, I pushed my hair back. "What do you want to hear?"

"Everything," Olah encouraged.

"Okay." I braced myself. "I think I like him, but there's a major problem: Noel. He just told me less than ten minutes ago he basically wanted a mom and that he wanted said mom to be me," I said, spilling it in one breath and screwing my face up. "I'm so sorry," I said when they all gaped at me. "Now I'm too scared to pursue anything with Cupid because I don't want Noel to get hurt and I'd be the prime reason for that."

"Holy shit," Alex whispered, leaning back. "That's not what I expected."

"I don't *think* I like Cupid. I *know* I like Cupid," I explained, my eyebrows drawing inwards. "He's sweet and funny and helpful, and he gets nervous around me sometimes. He has the cutest smile ever, you don't understand. I melt every time I see it. He's such a great father too, and Noel really looks up to him, which shows a happy family dynamic." I paused for a breath before continuing. "This morning, I woke up to Cupid knocked out at the foot of the bed and then Noel joined us in bed, and I realized this is what I want. I want a family but not just any family. I want them." I buried my head in my hands and tears started to present themselves. "I'm going to hurt everyone, aren't I?"

"Nice." Blinking away my tears, I peered up at Cece, whose lips stretched into a massive grin. "Noel warmed up to you, and Cupid fancy's you."

"Huh?"

"Noel doesn't warm up to people too quickly," Olah elaborated. "The kid's only six, but he has a clear sixth sense on who to trust and who not to trust. He gets it from his father. There have been two times where Cupid's introduced a woman to him, and both times, he's thrown a fit and refused to warm up even after multiple meetings, so Cupid let them go, and after the second one, he just stopped."

"He made me babysit Noel," I said plainly.

"I know," Alex said, shaking her head in disbelief. "I still can't wrap my head around that. Every time I ask, he mumbled out some pathetic excuse, but I honestly don't know why he did it."

Did Cupid want to see how his son would interact with me? Was that possible? But at that point, we hadn't even known each other well.

"As for Cupid, he's clearly protective over you," Alex continued. "And no woman ever left him tongue-tied or flustered that way you do, so yes, I do think you have a really good chance."

They all stared at me expectantly, and I stared back, lost for words.

"Now what?" I asked. "Do I confess my underlying love for him and then propose we elope and live together forever and then be buried together in one casket while holding hands?"

They all shared a laugh. "I hope Lyco knows just how crazy you are," Olah said, shaking her head.

"Don't confess," Alex advised. "He'll only run away like a big baby, and also, for the love of God, don't elope. I'll kill both of you."

"Definitely not eloping," I said with a nod. "I want a cute wedding."

"You guys are getting ahead of yourselves," Cece interrupted, pulling the blanket closer to her. "They aren't even dating yet."

"Right, right, but it's still fun to think about."

A knock on the door strayed out attention. "It's Lyco," Alex said, getting to get her feet.

"Wait," I cried. "What do I do?"

"Make him admit first, and before he flees, make sure he knows how you feel and what your future plans are. He needs a forever with you, not just a maybe," Alex finalized before walking away.

Olah squeezed my leg encouragingly. "You got this. You'll be married within days."

Cece winked at me. "I better be a bridesmaid."

"Bridesmaid?" all our heads snapped to the door, where Cupid was looking at us over Alex's shoulder. His eyes settled on me, vacant of all emotions.

"Long story," I said nervously, getting to my feet and walking towards him.

He thought over my answer, clear dissatisfaction on his face, but he changed the subject. "I got a few things to do, so I came to ask if you wanted a ride home or if you're staying," he said with a new edge to his voice I wasn't fond of.

"Nah, I should go," I said, turning to the girls. "I got a few things to redo at home, but I honestly had so much fun. Thank you!"

They all said their farewells, and I waved over my shoulder as I stepped into the hall with him. Noel already escaped the hallway and rolled into Alex's apartment with a truck full of toys. When the door closed behind us, Cupid blocked my way towards his place. I know if I told him to move, he would, but I didn't. Something told me this was going to lead to an interesting conversation.

"Yes?" I asked, peering up at him.

"Are you still seeing Thor?" Cupid asked, pinning me with scrutinizing eyes.

"What?" I asked, staring with wide eyes. "No. What're you talking about?"

"Don't lie to me, Sophia."

"I'm not!" I argued, wrapping my arms around my stomach and trying to keep myself upright. What was he on about?

"You've only been seeing one person, which is Thor," he stated. "When you told me you'd find someone on your own, did you mean Thor?"

"Well, yes but—"

"So, are you still seeing him?"

"Cupid, you're not listening to me!" I cried, the frustration building and exploding in my chest. Why were my words falling upon deaf ears? "Let me ex—"

"You explained it loud and clear. You're still hung up over Thor, despite everything he's done to you. I heard you talking just now about marrying him."

My jaw dropped, and my mind blanked. "What are—who—no, Cupid…wait, that's not—it's not what it seemed like!"

"Then tell me," he demanded, turning away and walking to his room. He pushed his door open with an airy touch. I followed him inside and found my neatly folded dress put on top of the cupcake tray with a familiar jagged paper he often wrote on about my upcoming dates. He snatched it off and crumbled it up, hiding it in his palm.

What do I tell him? What do I say? Cupid, it's you I want to marry! No, he'd disappear from the face of the Earth and never talk to me again. "Its just…I…" I stumbled on my words, not forming coherent sentences.

"That's what I thought," he said under his breath. "Grab your stuff. I'll drop you home."

"No, no, no, you have to listen to me. You don't understand. You don't understand," I repeated over and over, stalling so I could correctly word what I wanted to tell him. "Cupid, it's you—"

"Sophia, I don't want to hear your excuses. If you love Thor, then so be it. It just means I get to keep my job and we don't have to deal with each other, alright?"

"Wh…wait, what?" That hurt. "You'd honestly leave me just like that?"

Thor was right.

"Yes, I'm only here for a job, remember?" he reminded me, raising an eyebrow and looking at me like I was stupid.

"That's it? I was really just a job to you?" I asked, hurt coloring my words. It was hard to conceal it.

My god, Thor was right.

"Yes, Sophia," he answered, his voice holding a familiar hard edge.

"Then why did you string me along? Why did you have to introduce me to your family?" No matter how much air I tried to suck in, nothing could get to my airway.

"I didn't string you along," he answered, his tone turning bored and his calculating eyes becoming tired. "My job consisted of reintroducing the seven types of Greek love to you. It was your personal choice to get close."

"That's not true!"

"Yes, it is. You invited me for dinner, and called me during heartache, and asked me to help around the house," he said flatly. "I didn't volunteer nor ask for any of it."

"But you agreed to it…" I couldn't believe my ears.

"For the last time, Sophia," he drawled out like I wouldn't process simple words. "It's my job. I have to keep you satisfied and happy."

Thor was right.

"Really?" I whispered, feeling defeated. "You have no feelings for me? Not even as a friend?"

"No."

That cold, one-word answer ruined me. I grabbed the cupcake tray and dress, head bowed. "I can call an Uber."

"No, I'll drive you," he finalized opening the door and letting me out first. "Let's go."

I sat in the back seat, not wanting to be anywhere near him if I could help it. When he dropped me off, I left without a word, into the comfort of my house and the comfort of my bed, where I lay for the rest of the day, drowning in my own tears.

Love hurts.

23

Mistakes After Mistakes

Monday, February 8

With a pounding headache and red-rimmed eyes, I called into work, refusing to leave the comfort of my bed. I buried myself under blankets and stuffed my face into my pillow for another few hours, drifting in and out of sleep with Sirus curled up right beside me.

"Please don't ever leave me," I whispered, holding Sirus close to my chest, and she didn't protest once. She just cuddled closer and blinked at me.

She meowed, and I took that as her promise.

I couldn't help but laugh at my own stupidity. I should have gone with my guts and left him alone. All I did was hurt everyone involved, like the curse I am. All the signs were there, and I still ignored them. He resembled the man that broke into my house, truly portraying his real self.

Cupid made it clear from the beginning that he needed me to fall in love so he could keep his job. Then, he proceeded to talk shit about me every chance he got. Lubin mentioned that Cupid always came home frustrated and confused after spending time with me, which meant the time he did spend with me, all smiles and jokes, was for show. He was no better than Thor. I didn't know why I thought otherwise.

After I woke for the third time, I dragged my phone close to me, unblocked Thor's phone number, and called him. I listened to it ring a few times before going to voicemail.

"Thor," I whispered hoarsely into the phone. "You were right. I don't know what to say besides you were right. Cupid was using me, and when he got what he wanted, he left me. Please…please forgive me. I'll be waiting for you by the grocery store near my house at 6:30 if you choose to come listen to me. I can't express how sorry I am."

Sirus licked my cheek as more tears rushed down.

Maybe I was just a stupid fool but at least I'd be a stupid fool who wouldn't die alone.

By the time the clock turned 6:30, I stood outside the grocery store, dressed as close to nice as I could. I forced myself to put on makeup to hide the red-rimmed eyes and the blotchy face, but makeup could only do so much.

By 6:45, I was losing hope but stuck it out.

By 6:50, I texted Thor twice.

By 7:00, I admitted to being a woman without dignity.

Just as I was about to leave, a familiar car pulled up in front of me, and the windows rolled down. Thor smirked at me while taking a long sip of his drink.

"Get in," he said after he swallowed.

I licked my lips, wondering if this was the right decision. Pulling open the door, I slid in and watched him put his drink into the cup holder.

"Hey," I whispered, brushing my hair back and avoiding his eyes.

"Hey yourself," he said with a smooth chuckle, pulled into the further, emptier end of the parking lot, and parked. "So, why did you want to see me?"

My pulse picked up, and I ground down on my teeth. "I told you over voicemail." Why was I doing this again?

He cocked an eyebrow. "You'll just have to remind me, Sweetheart."

"I…need…you." I almost choked on the words. All I could replay was his fisted hands and his rage-fueled face when he found Cupid and me on my kitchen floor.

"Sorry, what? I couldn't hear you," he said, his lips curving up high as he leaned in.

'I need you to make the best decision for your mental health and for your future, okay?'

Maybe I didn't have to do this. Cupid would understand, right?

"I…"

No, Cupid would lose his job and he would never forgive me.

"Need…"

Screw Cupid. Screw the thirty other people who wouldn't fall in love because of me. Screw love.

"No one."

Picking up his drink, I popped off the lid and dumped it all over his smug face.

As Cupid once said, *'You deserve happiness, love, care, security.'*

"I need no one," I spat. The smug look on his face slid away with the sticky drink. He vomited out incoherent words while trying to blink the liquid out of his eyes. "I don't care what you have to say. That's why I called you here, Thor. Because you can suck my toes for all I care. I don't need Cupid, I don't need love, and I sure as hell don't need you! I'll do fine just on my own! I have come this far without any of you, and I'll get even further!"

"You bitch!" In lightning speed, he locked the door and had me pinned face-down against the dashboard with my hands behind my back. "You're going to pay for that!"

"I'm not paying for shit!" I yelled back, trashing in his hold. The grip slipped enough for me to loosen one hand. My heartbeat pounded in my chest, ear, throat, and fingers. I could feel it pulsing in every part of my body, knowing I might not get out of his car alive. He twisted my one arm higher up, making me cry out.

"I tried to do you a favor by giving you another chance with me, and this is how you behave? I've never come across someone so ungrateful!" he roared, applying force onto my back.

My fingers skimmed my keychain, but when he shifted me again, pain exploded in my shoulder and made me see stars.

"LET GO OF ME! HELP ME! AHH!"

He grabbed my hair and jerked me back. He forced me to stare at his deranged face and wild eyes.

My god, why did I get in the car? Why did he have to park this far in the parking lot? I needed help. I was going to die. He was going to ruin me.

My fingers skimmed the rough fabric of my keychain again, and I forced my fingers to wrap around them, unsure if I even managed to get a good grasp on it due to the lack of blood flowing to my fingers and numbing them.

The muscles I once loved were now working against me. Even the slightest amount of force he used made me feel like all my bones were damn near close to cracking.

"I'm not going to hurt you," he spat. "I'm going to do something better. The next time you see *Cupid,* it'll be in the hospital." He actually spat on me. He balled up saliva and, *tuk,* spat right on my face, nailing me in one eye.

Not only was I a screaming mess, I was a mess who could only see with one eye. I thrashed even harder, only as a momentary distraction before I finally untangled my free hand and felt around for the pepper spray.

"What the—" he spotted it just as it slipped right through my fingers and onto the mat.

"NO!" I screamed as he dove for it, no longer restraining me. I kicked upwards with my toes, skimming his jaw but it was hard enough to distract him. I popped opened the lock and stumbled out, yanking the key chain with my foot as I did. I fumbled for a moment, unable to hold it in between my butter fingers long enough, giving Thor the advantage of righting himself. His foot leaned out, ready to get out and pounce, but my finger finally found the paper spray and I squeezed, aiming anywhere I could, and when I heard the sound of his satisfying painful scream, I squeezed for a few seconds longer before I finally let up and leaned heavily against the open door.

Thor retreated into the car, clawing at his face and screaming profanities. Leaning in, I grabbed his ear and pulled him to me with a sharp tug. "Next time, it'll be a taser. I carry that with me too, so don't think about ever seeing me again, you understand?"

He was too busy crying to respond, and so, I left him, knowing he was smart enough to back down. At least, I hoped he was.

I stood with steady legs despite my whole insides quivering. I slammed the door shut, kicking it for good measure, and then strode my way out of the parking lot as fast as I could, glancing back a few times.

I stopped by a payphone and called the police station, telling them about a lunatic in the back end of the parking lot of the grocery store, trying to lure children in. That should do for now.

The walk home allowed for the adrenaline to melt away, leaving my ecstatic, pulsing thoughts a trail of water behind me. All my energy evaporated by the time I was on my front steps, heaving in and out.

The pain wasn't as bad either. Although he had been adding force, he didn't do anything damaging. He restrained my arm in the worst way possible but nothing that would leave any permanent marks or that needed immediate care. I did bet on a bruise forming on my forehead, though.

With a tired, defeated sigh, I slumped down on the front chair and stretched my legs out. Despite feeling like I set the world on fire, I couldn't help a small, satisfied smile. I could take care of myself just fine, and Thor would know better than to mess with me again.

As for love…I realized what I said in the car was true.

I didn't need Thor.

I didn't need Cupid.

I didn't need love.

It felt nice finally coming to terms with something that weighed heavily on me for so long. It was okay if I didn't fall in love because I didn't need it to survive.

I was more than happy to acknowledge that I wanted it, though.

I wanted to love.

I wanted Cupid.

Both of those combined gave me eternal happiness.

Pulling out my phone, I called Cupid's number. He may have said some hurtful things, but he did deserve to know whether he'd get fired or not. When it took me to voicemail, I said, "I didn't end up finding my compatible partner. I'm sorry for costing you your job."

Then I sat back and allowed myself to be happy with decisions for the first time in a long time. It also helped knowing Thor was probably in handcuffs sitting in the back of a police car right now.

24

Heart Eyes

Tuesday, I called in at work and decided I needed another day to recover. Just one more day and then I was done hiding. Although I came to terms with myself, there was still a second part to this mess that made me sad. I had to let go of Lubin, Noel, Alex, Olah, and Cece. They had intertwined themselves in my life in such a positive, uplifting way that now, I just felt lonely. At least I knew I had my family, especially Elena, who I'd been too embarrassed to call.

At some point during the evening, someone knocked on the door, but I ignored it. When the door creaked open, I figured I might die tonight.

"Sophia!" Cupid called, his voice ringing through the empty house. This was worse than death. Was he here to twist the knife he stabbed me with?

I lay motionless under my blanket, staring blankly at the door.

Please leave. Please, for the love of God, just leave me alone.

He didn't leave. He started downstairs, looking through all the rooms before making his way upstairs, where he eventually found my body hidden under the blanket.

"Sophia," he called, distant enough for me to know he hadn't entered the room. "I need to talk to you."

"I'm sorry for making you lose your job," I mumbled.

"No, I didn't lose my job," he said, not making a move to get any closer. His voice remained cold, just like the first time we met and the last time we spoke. "In fact, when I went to resign, the committee informed me that the charts showed I did my job."

"I don't understand," I mumbled.

"It means you fell in love and so did the man you were courting," he said, not speaking Thor's name. He chuckled softly, but there was no humor in it. "The charts calculate the positive emotions, along with the love that the individuals hoard. They said yours went from close to negative to ninety-three percent over the last twenty-four days, and there was a significant hike in your significant other's chart as well."

"Wh—what?" I stuttered, pulling the blanket away from my face and sitting up, my face draining of all color.

"They said you have work to do to make the relationship steady, but I still did my job in uniting you with a compatible match." He hummed. "Although, I have you to thank for that part since you did find him, after all." Our eyes met from across the room; they were as empty as before. I wish they'd spark with some form of emotion, whether it be anger, or humor, or sadness. "So, I came by to say thanks for saving my job and I wish you the best of luck with…*him.*" Disgust. There was disgust in his voice.

Then he turned, giving me his broad back, and started his walk down the dark hallway but paused before he got too far. Without turning around, he said, "I just want to see you happy."

I didn't lose my job…the charts showed I did my job…you fell in love, and so did the man you were courting…significant hike in your significant other's chart…

"Sirus," I mumbled, lifting her curled-up body and placing her on my legs. "This doesn't make sense."

Did he mean…there's no way. Wait, maybe there *was* a way. No, no, that wasn't possible. How could that be possible? He made it clear it was work. He made it clear I meant nothing to him. Unless…

Not only did Alex tell me that Cupid had feelings for me, but the charts said the same thing. Cupid was, after all, the only man I had eyes for.

My head dropped onto my pillow with a groan as realization dawned on me.

Cupid only had eyes for me, too.

25

Bruised Toes

Friday, February 12

The night Cupid left, I finally crawled out of bed and started working on a game plan to get back the insecure man with a wall around his heart. Cupid proved to be a hard man. Getting him back was going to take a lot of work, but with the help of Pinterest and my imagination, I got it done in three days.

The backyard needed major maintenance. I spent one whole day working on mowing the grass, picking out the weeds, and fixing the wooden fence. I also took care of the back deck that had been collecting dust and practically rotting.

On day two, I spent my day shopping for the materials I would need to woo Cupid. The process consisted of a lot of back and forth driving between several stores because I kept forgetting to pick out something from one store or the other and having to go back. It was that day I had an odd encounter.

I made a pit stop by the cosmetic isle. I promised myself I wouldn't splurge on things I didn't know how to use, but I found myself contemplating buying an eyebrow pencil. I looked at the different shades, wondering if I should go darker or lighter than my eyebrow shade.

"Excuse me."

"Oh, sorry," I apologized, stepping out of the man's way.

He stepped in front of me, picked up an eyebrow pencil in a shade I hadn't contemplated and turned back to me. "This will suit you well. Your eyebrows are dark enough, but this will help fill them in if you please," he said, holding it out to me.

"Oh…" I grabbed it after a second of hesitation. "Thank you."

"No worries, Sophia." His bow-shaped lips curved up in a warm smile while my mouth fell open. "I assume this is part of the plan in getting Lyco back?"

"How do you—why—who are you?" I stammered over my words, trying to find the best question to ask the gorgeous man in front of me that resembled someone I'd looked up far too much this last month.

"Oh, how rude of me." He put out his hand for me to shake. "I'm Cupid. The real Cupid. It's a pleasure to meet you." My hand fell into his, but I was too in awe to really shake it as I stared at the curly-haired, baby-faced man with tattoos peeking out of his collar. "Back to business. How's everything with Lyco going? I took a look at his charts this morning and saw everything was going according to plan, except for one thing."

I tilted my head. "What's going according to plan?"

"My plan to make him fall in love with you, of course."

"I thought…well, Cupid—my Cupid—I mean not my Cupid but Lyco…anyways, Lyco said that he's in charge of finding his own soulmate."

"Yeah, he is, but he's so focused on everyone else, he let his own love life go and who better than you to remind him of it?"

"A million other women," I point out.

The real Cupid paused for a moment, his eyes following a woman who walked past us, holding up two facewashes. Once she was gone, Cupid spoke again. "No, you're the perfect fit for him, and while he's great at spotting love for others, he's not so great when it comes to himself. When I assigned you for him ten years ago, I didn't think it'd take him this damn long, my god."

"Wait, this is a setup?"

"Of course, of course. You did well on your part not falling for anyone, but Lyco was terrible at it, so I got the committee to come down hard on him."

"Lyco said it's because he fools around a lot and they're just looking for any excuse to kick him off."

The real Cupid scoffed. "When you're in my good grace, nothing gets you kicked off…but don't tell him that or he'll just act out more. Anyways, it was all going according to plan and Lyco is usually careful when he does his job, making sure to do everything according to plan, which includes checking the files every time they're updated. Unfortunately, he got too cocky with your file since he seemed to think he knew you inside and out. So, he never checked your file anymore, which means he thinks you're in love with Thor."

"Which is exactly why I'm going to talk to him tomorrow," I stated.

"I know." He looked pointedly at my cart filled with decorations. "Anyways, good luck." He started walking away, hands tucked in his pockets and whistling an odd tune.

"Good luck with what?" I asked, following after him. "You're not foreshadowing failure, are you?"

"Good luck with Lyco. That boy is a handful." He turned the corner. When I caught up and looked around the shelf, there was not a figure in sight. I glanced around, wondering if I had just hallucinated.

The encounter was odd, but in a comforting way.

At last, on the third day, I got to work blowing balloons, setting up the table and chairs, and cooking. By early evening, I stood in my backyard, hands on my hips and gazing at my hard work. No man had ever been deserving of such efforts from me, so all I could think was that Cupid better appreciate it.

The sun was just minutes shy of setting, softening the sky with cotton candy colors. The fairy lights set up around the backyard failed to glow to the best of their ability but once the sun set, they would glow bright and illuminate the table set with a red cover, petals of red and pink flowers, small candles, and our plate and glass. The helium-filled, heart-shaped balloons loitered around the table and backyard. The bouquet of red and pink roses in the middle of the table pulled everything together wonderfully.

The doorbell ringing brought me out of my nervous haze. Jogging inside the house, I opened the door and beamed at the women in front of me.

"Thank you so much," I said excitedly, moving aside to allow the girls to pile in with bags and bags of tools. "I want to look good."

"You already look good," Cece said kindly. "We're just going to enhance what you have."

"Lyco won't be able to take his eyes off you," Olah said, throwing an arm around my shoulder and pulling me with her.

"He'll fall to his knees," Alex said with a snicker as we made our way upstairs. "I'm glad you're fighting for what you want."

For the next half hour, Cece worked on my hair, Alex worked on my face, and Olah worked on my nails while I told them everything that happened since I left Alex's place. They listened and gave their input.

They didn't let me look until I got into my dress that practically fits like a second skin. I had to admit, it was the most beautiful, extravagant thing I owned. The straps were off the shoulder and the dress fell to the floor with a slit down my left leg. The sweetheart neckline worked perfectly with the necklace that settled just above the breasts. The satin finish pulled it all together, matched beautifully with the glossy red nails.

The girl's jaws touched the floor when I stepped out of the bathroom and into their line of sight.

"Holy shit," Alex whispered. "Can't I just have you?"

Olah tucked her hair behind her ears as her eyes slowly took me in. "How about you skip out on Lyco and I take you on a date?"

"You don't even go for girls," Alex scoffed, elbowing her.

Cece did a dance of victory, her body radiating nothing but happiness. "Lyco is one lucky man. Not only are you stunning on the inside, but you're sexy on the outside too," she said, stopping in front of me.

"Alright, look in the mirror now!" Alex said excitedly. "Assuming you didn't peak in the bathroom."

"Promise I didn't," I said, nervously wringing my fingers together and turning around.

My full-length mirror gave me a startling view. "Wow," I mumbled as I took in my whole appearance. The dress truly did hug every inch of my body in the most flattering way possible, giving me curves I was sure I didn't have. Olah had pinned my curled hair into an elegant updo with ringlets of loose curls falling out. My makeup tied everything together with a sizzle. The red eye makeup made my eyes rounder and entrancing. The red glitter sparkled under the light, matching the bright red lip color that looked close to dripping with its beautiful glossy shine. Everything else, like foundation, concealer, highlight, blush, and bronzer truly did enhance my features without looking caked.

"I don't know what to say," I said, turning to face the girls, who had small smiles on their lips. "Thank you so much."

"Don't thank us," Alex said, waving me away and continuing to pack up the remainder of their things. "We were more than happy to help."

"No, Alex," I said, guilt settling in my stomach. "I really owe you for this. I know you won't take money, but is there anything I can do?"

Cece stood up and gave me a look that made me flinch back. I didn't know she was capable of such a soul-burning look. "This is what friends do," she drawled out slowly. "Get used to it, Sophia. We're here for you."

As tears glossed my eyes, Olah said, "Don't cry! You'll ruin your makeup."

"I love you guys so much," I whispered with true sincerity.

"We know," Alex said, flipping her hair and giving me a wink. "Cupid should be here in five minutes. I told him I needed a ride."

"Can you tell him to come to the backyard?" I asked, starting to fidget with my fingers. My pulse hummed out of control, threatening to put me in the hospital if I didn't calm down. For the last three days, all I could think about was what I'd say to him. Now that the time had come, I blanked.

"Yes, I'll make something up," she said, and her eyes met mine. I noticed hers had also started to become glossy. "God, I'm so happy for that man. He truly did find someone wonderful." She gasped and reached into her pocket. "I almost forgot!" She pulled out a crumpled paper, flattened it out and handed it to me. "I found this on Lyco's counter."

Delicately taking it out of her hands, I recognized it as the same one he snatched off my dress during our heated argument in his condo.

Lyco King

5793 Larton Ave

6:00 pm

"What…what is this?" I stuttered as my heart slammed against my ribcage. "Was he going to ask me on a date?"

"Seems like it," Alex said with a giggle.

"Alright, let's go," Olah encouraged, and they all piled out while I continued to stare blankly at the paper.

Wonderful.

After helping me set up the food outside, they wished me luck and left me to my daunting thoughts as I paced the backyard in heels I had no business wearing. The sky dimmed into soft darkness and sparing clouds loomed above, promising to cry with me if the date went south. The fairy lights worked their true magic in illuminating the backyard, which only made my heartbeat increase. The set up looked romantic, but there's nothing romantic about sweat stains under the pits.

As I adjusted the chairs for the seventeenth time, someone cleared their throat behind me. With a startled gasp, I spun around and found Cupid standing there, looking like a model off the runway.

"Whoa," I mumbled, catching my lip between my teeth and tasting the overpowering flavor of gloss, as my eyes took in the hunk of a man before me. He stood tall in a fitted suit that only made him look larger and more fit than he already was, along with a tie that matched my dress. He styled his hair back without a strand out of place, and his scuff of a beard was lined neatly.

When my eyes lifted to meet his, I found his eyes still taking me in, his lips parted and his eyes wide. His gaze left a trail of fire on every part he took in, making me feel on top of the world. When his eyes met mine, he seemed dazed and lost for words.

"You-you…uh…wow," he breathed out, his eyebrows rising in disbelief. "You look stunning, Sophia."

The smile came naturally, and I lowered my gaze, feeling my face heat up. "Thank you," I mumbled.

Another moment of silence stalled our conversation before Cupid cleared his throat. "Am I interrupting something?" he asked awkwardly, taking a step back. "Alex told me to pick her up from here. I didn't mean to barge in."

"Oh…" I trailed off. I figured Alex must have slipped him some information considering he was wearing a tux. "No, Cupid. I set this up for us."

I left him struggling for an answer as I walked to my phone and speaker to put on soft, slow music suggested by Lubin. Mustering up all the courage I had, I walked over to him, taking his large hand in mine, and leading him to the table, where our dinner awaited.

"I don't understand," Cupid said after a moment, once I served him and myself.

"Cupid, it's you," I said, keeping my eyes focused on my plate. "When you spoke about the charts that said I fell for a man who returned my feelings, it was you. The only man I've fallen for is you."

When his answer buffered, I finally raised my eyes to look at him and found him still in a state of daze. "You're lying," he said, his voice cracking slightly. He cleared his throat. "Sorry."

A giggle slipped before I could stop it, and Cupid shot me a playful glare. "I'm not. I don't know if I love you, but I do know I see a future with you."

"So, you do love me," he said, now taking a teasing approach. "You only see futures with those you truly are in love with."

"Alright, Mr. Love, take it easy," I said, giving him a light kick under the table. "We're not even dating." I titled my head. "But we could be."

"Oh…" Cupid trailed off, and my mood dampened again.

"Oh, come on, Cupid," I said, letting my impatience show. "What are you scared of? Hell, I'm a lot more scared than you are and not only did I set this up, but I even asked you out. Throw me a bone here, please."

Cupid took a bite of dinner, and I did the same, waiting for his well thought-out response. "I hate to admit it, but I'm scared of a lot of things when it comes to love, alright, Sophia? I watched my dad die from heartbreak, and I'm watching my pa struggle to find a reason to live. Love is one hell of a drug I'm not ready to take, especially one that may also hurt Noel."

"I understand that, but there are some risks you're going to have to take when you fall for someone," I explained. "You should know that. You're Cupid. I think I've shown just how intertwined I am with you and your life."

"That's the scary part," he said, his lips tugging up in a weary smile. "You're so invested. Noel loves you, and my family has adapted to you so much that there's always a mild conversation about you when we're all together. And…" He hesitated. "And I've never felt so down and lonely and lost after our fight. You're bound to damage me."

Unable to help it, I grinned. "You felt down, lonely, and lost? I felt like my heart was ripped out of my chest, and no man as ever had this effect on me in the twenty-six years I've lived, which is how I just know you're the one."

"You're the one, too," he admitted, his eyes softening. "Just promise you won't hurt me."

I put out my pinky. "As long as you promise it back."

He looped his pinky with mine, and we both whispered, "I promise."

"Now tell me, why are you wearing the tux?" I asked when we settled back to eating.

"Alex told me she needed me for a meeting, but I had to dress nice. She gave me the tie," he answered after swallowing. "This is a lot. You didn't have to do it."

"I wanted to," I said with honesty. "You brought a lot of happiness and comfort back into my life that I rejected. You opened my eyes to how terribly I've been acting with my family, and while I'm sure there's a long way to go, it's definitely a start. I do owe you a lot for that."

"You don't owe me anything," he said, shaking his head. "I liked it. I liked seeing you happy and whole again."

That made me tilt my head slightly. "When did you know you liked me?"

His lips tilted up slightly while capturing my eyes and holding them. "The second I laid eyes on you. The day you entered your house, talking to your cat about a stepdad, I found humor and lightheartedness from the woman I pegged as stubborn, dark, and lonely. Then you jokingly flirted with me the second day, and for some reason, I couldn't stop thinking about you. It only made it harder when Pa approved of you and Alex wouldn't stop rambling about how wrong I was about you."

"Then Noel," I said.

"Then Noel," he agreed. "It was never part of the plan and then, suddenly, it was. If Noel approved, maybe I could give it a try. After the day he spent with you, I asked how he felt about you, and while he was being stuck up about it, I did notice he was softer and didn't reject the idea of seeing you again."

"So, why didn't you just come out and date me?" I asked curiously. "Would have saved us a lot of time."

"I can't even fathom the thought of dating you right now," he pointed out. "Imagine how paranoid I was after only talking to you for a few days. You were playful and kind by nature, so I didn't read anything into it and figured you wouldn't return the feelings anyway."

"Wow, you're so dense. There wasn't even a moment where you thought, 'Huh, maybe she's flirting with me?'" I asked, intrigued.

"Of course, there was the time at the bakery when you asked me on a date, but then I thought it was all in my head. There was also the time you invited me over to help paint and made dinner and dessert, but I figured you saw me as nothing but a friend," he said with a lift of his shoulder. "You're hard to read."

"I think we both suck at reading each other," I said with a grin as we scrapped the last of our food. Cupid had taken seconds, making me feel like a better chef than Gordan Ramsey.

When I put my fork down, Cupid put his hand out for me. "Will you do me the honor of dancing with me?" he asked in a posh accent.

With a giggle, I slipped my hands into his, and he led me into the opening, the music softly wrapping around our bodies as he took the lead.

"Cupid?" I whispered as we swayed under the bright moonlight and smiling stars.

"Yes?"

"I don't know how to take care of a child."

"I don't know how to take care of a cat."

I smiled. "We'll just teach each other then."

After a moment of warm silence, Cupid whispered, "Sophia?"

"Cupid."

"Please don't stop laughing. I can't get enough of it."

"As long as you don't stop smiling. I'm addicted."

Our faces moved in close, and our lips met in the middle. Fireworks didn't go off nor did my feet leave the ground, but his arms felt like home, and life seemed to make a little more sense.

The clouds came together then and drizzled droplets of happy tears. When I got a closer look at the droplets trailing down Cupid's face, I noticed the prominent shape of hearts. I looked up at the sky and smiled, hoping the real Cupid felt my gratitude. We spent the remainder of the night laughing and smiling while he taught me more slow dance moves and I bruised his toes.

I wouldn't have it any other way.

$$26$$

Happy Valentine's Day

Sunday, February 14

There was no better way of spending Valentine's Day than spending it with the people you love dearly. It may have taken twenty-six years to realize that and find those people, but if there's one thing Cupid taught me, it's that it's never too late.

"The house looks beautiful!" Elena cried as her eyes took in what little she could see from the entrance.

"Of course, it does," I said smugly before we kissed each other's cheeks. "Hey, baby, how's life been treating you?" I asked my little niece, hiking her onto my hips and kissing her as well.

She giggled, showing me her little teeth before she left a sloppy kiss of her own on my cheeks. "Good!" she cried and then squirmed, trying to get out of my hold. I let her down with one more kiss.

"What's up, in-law?" I asked Malcolm when he stepped through the door, holding roses.

"The roof," he answered with the lame answer only his lame self could produce. I laughed because I loved my lame in-law and I loved his lame jokes. He and my sister were perfect for each other.

We embraced before the small family moved along, allowing room for my grandma and parents.

"LOLA!" I cried, wrapping my arms tightly around the little woman. "I missed you."

"Clearly not enough if you never came to see me," she said, playfully hitting my head.

"Not fair. I've been busy," I said and kissed her as Mom and Dad stepped in behind her. "Wow, Dad, didn't think you could clean up nice."

"He can't," Mom said flatly. "I still dress him."

"And I undress you. Fair enough," Dad said, making my jaw drop and Mom slap his neck. The playful tone didn't go amiss by me, and I stared at him in awe. After Dad and I hugged, he left to help Lola.

"What?" I whispered into Mom's ear when we hugged.

"He's taken it easy on the drinking since that dinner, and he's been going religiously to those AA meetings. Maybe you are the favorite after all," she said, pulling away a little so we were still embracing, but she could see my eyes now. "I love you, Sophia."

"Obviously, I'm the favorite after all," I said with a wide grin.

She pinched my side, leaving me laughing and greeting the next guests.

"Oh, carpooling!" I called out the door, peering at the twins as they got out of their car with their girlfriends. "I see that you've taken it upon yourself to care for the environment."

Quinn and his girlfriend, Amanda, came up the steps first. He greeted me with a hard punch to the arm, making me wince.

"You idiot, that hurt," I snapped, reaching for his hair, but he easily deflected.

"Nice try, furball," he said, stepping past me and into the house.

"Damn, where'd you get that dress?" Amanda asked, tucking her fiery red hair behind her ear as she took me in. "You look great!"

"Thank you!" I said. "I honestly don't remember the store name. It was online. I'll find it and send it to you, but you can borrow it whenever you want!" I liked Amanda. Her and Quinn had been dating for over two years and I was sure he was going to propose any day.

Wade and his girlfriend, Lidija, pulled me into a bear hug as they normally did when they were together. "How's my little sister-in-law?" Lidija asked teasingly.

"I'm older than you," I reminded, pulling myself free from their assaulting hug.

"By a month," she reminded.

"A month," Wade echoed, emphasizing his wife's words.

"How's the baby?" I asked as another car pulled up.

"Active," Wade said, suddenly beaming with pride as we glanced down at his wife's stomach.

"Way too much morning sickness," Lidija said. "Wait until you get pregnant and then we can bond," she called over her shoulder as they walked further into the house, leaving me to greet my older brother and his wife, Ester.

"My favorite people on Earth," I greeted. "How have you guys been?"

"Peachy," Ester answered, shooting Kai a glare. "Your brother forgot to get the gift off the counter before we came."

"A gift?" I asked, furrowing my eyebrows. "Honestly, it's a good thing he forgot it. I don't need anything."

"That's what I said," Kai said pointedly. When I punched his arm lightly, he chuckled and messed up my hair. We all stepped inside, and I was about to close the door when another car pulled up and out piled one too many people from a car that only sat five people.

My smile stretched impossibly far, and I listened to their loud voices echoing down the street. The girls were the first ones out and at the door, greeting me, hugging me, and complimenting everything in their line of sight. After they piled in, Lubin, Lyco, and Noel made their way up. Lubin gave me a firm handshake and a simple 'how are you?' before moving in, followed by Noel, who didn't even seem to see me as he rushed into the house after Lubin.

Lyco saved himself to be the last of my guest to finally enter, closing the door behind him. "The place looks great," he said, giving me a wink.

"I couldn't have done it without you, huh?" I asked, hooking my fingers into his belt loops and pulling him against me. "Did I get to say thank you?"

"You did, but I wouldn't mind if you said it again," he said, his eyes glinting as he stared down at me.

"Mm, well, *Cupid*, thank you for helping me set up the house and cooking dinner for our Valentine's party," I mumbled, getting on my toes, and letting my lips brush him.

"As long as I get to spend time with you, I don't care what I do," he mumbled back before capturing my lips with his.

In the living room, I found everyone mingling and getting along extremely well for two groups of people who never met before this day. The twins were playing card with Cece and Lilly. Olah was busy showing Lidija self-defense moves while Alex gave Ester tips on how to maintain her bleached hair. Grandma was busy talking Lubin's ear off, who seemed like he didn't mind listening, while Mom arm-wrestled with Noel. The others were talking or watching television, painting the red-and-pink-decorated house a pleasant, warm sight.

Walking over to the coffee table, I grabbed one of the pink heart-shaped cookies with 'ew' written on it and took a bite.

"The dessert table is great," Elena said, walking back with a doughnut from the doughnut tray with a label reading 'I doughnut know what I'd do without you.' "I went upstairs to use the bathroom and saw you finally set up your art room."

"Isn't it beautiful?" I asked excitedly, grabbing her hand and pulling her along with me upstairs. "I finished it up yesterday with Cupid, but I haven't had time to work on new projects."

"Do you plan on pursuing something in art?" she asked as I flickered on the light and we stood in the most important room in the house.

"I think I might start selling them online or maybe start an art blog or maybe a YouTube channel. I don't know, but what I do know is I can't wait to start painting again," I said honestly, turning to face Elena. She pulled me into a tight embrace.

"I'm so proud of you. I know you can do anything you put your mind to," she said, smoothing down my hair while pulling away. "I'm excited to see what you pull next."

"Probably shit out of my butt. I need to take a dump," I said, making her laugh and leave me alone. Truth is, I didn't want her to see my tears again. After collecting myself, I joined everyone downstairs, where we all continued to mingle and laugh and enjoy the presence of each other.

I busied myself with shuffling the cards for the next round of Uno. Each round, the group got bigger as new people joined and the more competitive it got. Mom decided to join this round.

"Are you joining?" Quinn asked Dad, who watched with a blank gaze.

He blinked twice, snapping out of whatever trance he was in. "I don't know how to play."

"Wade doesn't either and he's won twice," Quinn encouraged, making room between him and Wade for Dad to join. Wade stiffened slightly and Dad stared at his back for a moment. Then he opened his mouth to deny it again, but Wade spoke without turning to look at him.

"I'll help you," Wade said, grabbing half the deck from me. "Come join."

Dad's eyes seemed to soften, or maybe it was just the slight raise of his brows that shifted his expression, but he looked pleased nonetheless. He got off the couch and joined us on the floor. I handed the rest of the deck to Wade to hand out while leaning against Cupid's side.

Wade speaking five words to Dad was an improvement from the usual three words. They still may not be making eye contact and may still be sitting stiffly with each other, but it was a start.

The night slowed down after that, and we all lounged around after dessert, believing that all the excitement for the day passed, but Quinn proved us wrong when he got to his feet and called for attention.

"He's going to propose," I whispered to Cupid. "He has to, I know it."

"He is," Cupid confirmed. "Hate to brag, but I knew from the start of the night."

"No, you love to brag," I said, elbowing him and making him chuckle.

Noel crawled over to us and squeezed himself between us as Quinn grabbed Amanda's hand and knelt in front of her.

I gave Cupid a smug look. "Told you." Sirus pattered towards us when Noel encouragingly called for her. She pulled herself onto his small legs and curled up, making him grin.

"All I think about when I see you is that I can't wait to have a future with you, so Amanda, please have a future with me. Will you marry me?"

No one held their breath. We already knew the answer.

"About time!" Amanda cried, also getting on her knees and kissing Quinn. We all cheered for the happy couple, and I couldn't help sneaking a glance at Cupid while I captured Noel's hand in mine.

"That's going to be us one day," Cupid said, turning his eyes to me with a smile.

"I can't wait," I said with sparkling eyes and a wide smile. "By the way, Cupid, you never told me the last type of love."

His eyes held a spark of their own. "Pragma Love."

"Longstanding love," I cut in, ranking my fingers through his curls. "Longstanding love that comes from enduring hardship together and always committing to one another, often found between married couples. It's a love that comes with time and needs understanding, compromise, and tolerance."

"You did your research," he said, grabbing my hand and kissing the back of it. "But don't mix that up with an abusive, controlling relationship because those ups and downs are different from the average hardship found in a healthy relationship."

"Oh, don't I know it," I whispered.

I took a look around my room, slowly starting to list off the seven types of love surrounding me.

Searching the room, I found Mom and Dad cuddling on the couch, with Mom's head on Dad's shoulder and listing off household tasks that still need to be done. Dad just absentmindedly nodded while watching Lilly jump around. *Storge: Love of the child.*

My eyes found all the girls—Elena, Alex, Olah, Cece, Lidija, and Ester—surrounding Amanda and cooing over her ring and talking about the upcoming wedding. *Philia: Love of the mind.*

I looked at Grandma and Lubin, who were dancing to the sound of laughter and love in the middle of the living room. *Ludus: Playful love.*

I thought of my painting room and my future in doing what I love most. *Philautia: Love of the self.*

I thought about Tomas and the hospital hallways that Cupid filled with cheers and painted with bright colors of happiness. *Agape: Love of the soul.*

Returning my gaze to Cupid, my smile widened a little more. I may have had a bad Eros experience with the man from the bar, but something told me Cupid would make it memorable. *Eros: Love of the body.*

We may still be feeling out the relationship and finding our footing, but I knew this is the man I would climb mountains for and search the ends of the ocean for. *Pragma: Longstanding love.*

I settled my gaze on Noel's mop of curly hair and found his hand. I squeezed it three times.

Noel mimicked my move, unbeknownst to him what it meant.

I leaned down and whispered to Noel, "When you squeeze someone's hand three times, it means 'I love you'."

I expected him to pull his hand away and give me a dirty look only he was capable of. Instead, he grabbed Cupid's hand with his free one and dramatically squeezed both our hands three times at the same time.

When Cupid glanced down at him, Noel said, "I love you, Daddy." Noel looked at me. "I love you, Buttface."

Cupid and I looked at each other, our eyes silently communicating the words we had yet to say out loud.

I love you.

Acknowledgement

You know when you do something, and you can't believe you did it? That's how I felt when I survived a year of statistic and passed! Oh, and I also wrote a book! Writing the story itself was great, and now I get to write an acknowledgement? Wow. I still feel like I'm dreaming. There's a lot of people I have to thank for that.

I'd like to start by thanking the most important woman in my life: my mom. I didn't tell her about the book, but I kept showing her updated versions of the cover and she kept saying, 'why are you so impressed? It's not like you drew it.' Little did she know, her daughter was about to publish her first book. When I was younger, I always asked for a sister. I didn't realize I had one right here. Thank you for raising me with an unimaginable amount of love. She pushed me to do my best and believed I could do anything as long as I tried. Thank you.

Do you know that beautiful cover in the front? That was done by the one and only Tasneem Shaik. She spent endless hours putting it together and having the upmost patience I've ever seen in a person. 'Can you just…shift it to the right…no I mean left…wait can you centre it? Never mind, just put it back where it was.' Not only was she so incredibly patient, but she's just so sweet. She gives caramelized sugar a run for its money.

Here's to Maryam Desai, the woman I grew up with from birth. She watched me develop the immense amount of love I have for reading and writing and always encouraged me. She read my awful stories from middle school and never laughed. She always said she saw potential and as I wrote this book, she was always by my side, helping. She listened to me endlessly talk about the plot and the character and what I should do and what I shouldn't. Thank you.

Here's to Laila Sheather and Salaman Zafar, who gave their most honest opinions to help this book be what it is. I sent them drafts after drafts, interrupting mid-read and asking them to read the new copy instead. They listened to me go on and on about all aspects of my books and they always gave much-needed criticism. They were always there to give their impute, not a minute too late. I'll always be grateful for them having patience with me. Thank you.

Here's to my friends, Roha, Ayman, Fatima, Faiza, Noor, and Safura, who gave their feedback every time I asked. They also made me feel less lonely in this terrifying journey. Thank you.

I wanted to say a big thank you to Mrs. Chytra. She was a teacher at my high school, but I was never a student of hers. Two years after I graduated, I emailed her, asking if we could meet and she could tell me of her journey of becoming a published author of *Tarnished*. She was kind enough to meet me and talk to me about the process before and after publishing, the importance of beta readers, advertising, and everything in between. Ever the teacher, she gave a wonderful lesson. Thank you.

Last but not least, thank you. Thank you to the wonderful readers who got this far, whether you enjoyed it or not. Thank you for giving it a chance. Thank you for picking it up. Thank you for having faith. I appreciate you more than you will ever understand. Thank you.

Connect with Atika Desai

 : @atikadesai

 : @atikadesai

g : @atikadesai

www.atikadesai.com

About the author

Atika Desai is an author living in Toronto, Ontario. She is currently attending university to obtain her bachelor's degree in psychology and plans on becoming a teacher. She adores romance books for as long as she could remember and is happy to be able to write her own. When Atika is not writing, she is often reading romance or mystery novels, attempting new baking recipes, and procrastinating studying. She also enjoys spending her free time watching YouTube, listening to podcasts, and volunteering! *Cupid's Nightmare* is her debut novel.